CW01499862

Sympathy Tower Tokyo

Sympathy Tower Tokyo

RIE QUDAN

Translated by Jesse Kirkwood

**PENGUIN
VIKING**

VIKING

UK | USA | Canada | Ireland | Australia
India | New Zealand | South Africa

Viking is part of the Penguin Random House group of companies
whose addresses can be found at global.penguinrandomhouse.com

Penguin Random House UK,
One Embassy Gardens, 8 Viaduct Gardens, London SW11 7BW

penguin.co.uk

| Penguin
Random House
UK

First published in Japanese by Shinchosha 2024
This edition published by Viking 2025

002

Set in 11.5/14.5pt Dante MT Pro
Typeset by Jouve (UK), Milton Keynes
Printed and bound in Great Britain by Clays Ltd, Elcograf S.p.A.

The authorized representative in the EEA is Penguin Random House Ireland,
Morrison Chambers, 32 Nassau Street, Dublin D02 YH68

A CIP catalogue record for this book is available from the British Library

ISBN: 978-1-405-97206-2

Penguin Random House is committed to a sustainable future
for our business, our readers and our planet. This book is made from
Forest Stewardship Council® certified paper.

MIX
Paper | Supporting
responsible forestry
FSC® C018179

Translator's Note

The Japanese language relies on a combination of three distinct writing systems: kanji, hiragana and katakana. A central theme of *Sympathy Tower Tokyo* concerns the relationship between two of these in particular – kanji and katakana – and the reader may find a brief explanation of their key differences helpful.

Katakana is one of the two phonetic scripts (along with hiragana) in Japanese. It is primarily used for writing foreign words, names, onomatopoeia and scientific terms. Individual katakana characters represent sounds, rather than things or ideas, and visually are simpler and more uniform in structure than kanji. If you want to write 'coffee', you write コーヒー [kōhī], and each of those characters represents an approximation of a sound in the English word.

Kanji, on the other hand, are characters originally borrowed from Chinese, each carrying its own meaning, with pronunciation varying depending on the context. They are often used for nouns, verb stems, adjectives and Japanese proper names. The bad news for any student of Japanese is that they are much more complex visually and require memorization of thousands of characters to achieve fluency.

If you want to write 'green tea', you write 緑茶 [ryokucha], where the first character means 'green' and the second 'tea'.

The use of katakana became particularly widespread with the increasing use of foreign loanwords as Japan emerged from semi-isolation in the late nineteenth century. These days, their use is often associated with buzzwords, sales jargon, pop culture and a general desire to make things seem cool, modern, exciting, new. As our protagonist, Sara, notes, katakana-based words combine versatility and vagueness in a way that makes them an attractive choice for anyone wanting to avoid a firm commitment to meaning.

Speaking of Sara, her last name, Machina, is pronounced Makina – itself a plausible enough Japanese name, but one which she has chosen to spell in English with a 'ch'.

As for the Japanese name eventually given to the titular tower, Tōkyō-to Dōjō-tō, Sara is right to be astonished by the way it rolls off her tongue. The 'ō' sounds are drawn out, a bit like the 'aw' in the British pronunciation of 'law', while the unmarked 'o' is more staccato, a bit like the 'o' in the British pronunciation of 'not'. Reading aloud is strongly encouraged.

It would be Babel all over again. Sympathy Tower Tokyo would throw our language into disarray; it would tear the world apart. Not because, dizzy with our architectural prowess, we had reached too close to heaven and enraged the gods, but because we had begun to abuse language, to bend and stretch and break it as we each saw fit, so that before long no one could understand what anyone else was saying. The moment words left our mouths they would become to our listener a baffling tirade. A world ravaged by ranting. The era of the endless monologue.

In the gleaming black tiles of the bathroom where my reflection lurked, I was seeing the future again. Architects can always see the future. It reveals itself to us whether we like it or not.

Sympathy . . . Tower . . . Tokyo?

Of course, as architect, the building's name wasn't mine to decide, and whatever my misgivings I was hardly in a position to change it. And yet the moment the high-pressure jet of shower water hit my face, everything about that name

Sympathy Tower Tokyo
シンパシータワートーキョー

– the sound of it, the katakana characters used to approximate the English words, and what those words meant, and all the currents of power swirling around the project – started to bother me, and now there was no going back.

Before, it had simply been 'the Tower' in my mind, and that had been fine by me. Even after we were invited to submit a design, we'd been happy, at my firm, to simply refer to it as the 'Tower' project. Whatever it ended up being called, however bizarre or controversial the names eventually proposed to the public might be, that would have nothing to do with me. It had already taken shape inside me as the Tower. That was all it could signify. The Tower: nothing more and nothing less. As for its intended purpose, I'd already weighed my options and decided to avoid explicitly backing the project. Entering a design competition didn't have to mean the architect endorsed the ideas behind it. And yet the moment the Tower became 'Sympathy Tower Tokyo' it achieved a texture, a sort of sticky mucosity that I could feel adhering to the furrows of my brain. No amount of water could wash it away. From experience, I knew this to be a very bad sign.

Madness. What is? All of it. Isn't that going too far? Not far enough. Anyway, are you even allowed to call something 'madness' these days? Isn't that saneism? Let's just say they have a terrible sense for names, then. Who does? The Japanese people. Whoa, hang on. Isn't that a bit of a sweeping statement? Fine, then the Stakeholders . . . This was the frantic babble produced by the language-monitoring unit that had whirred automatically into life in my brain, even though it wasn't like anyone else was getting in there. Exhausted by the presence of the censor that had apparently taken up residence in my head, I felt a sudden, overwhelming desire for equations, for the rush of energy they'd supply. With equations, there was only one right answer. You didn't have to put yourself in the shoes of each of the numbers and adjust the solution accordingly. I longed for the equality of numbers, the soothing universality of their language. But there were no equations to be found in the bathroom. All I had for company in here was Sympathy Tower Tokyo and the Tower of Babel and the Stakeholders.

So: why, after thronging together and pooling their considerable wisdom and engaging in what must have been a long and considered discussion, had the Stakeholders settled on a name that sounded like that of a resort chain? Clearly, the very tone in which I was asking this question suggested that I perceived the project in a negative light. *Perceived it in a negative light?* Come on, let's be real: my entire being was instinctively screaming *no*, telling me the tower shouldn't exist. Every inch of my body was repelled by the incursion of the Sympathy Tower. Ah, I thought, now I know what this reminds me of. It reminds me of rape.

In the white noise of the shower I reassembled memories I'd long thought it unnecessary to retrieve. I had been raped. That was the fact of the matter. A boy much stronger than me had shoved my schoolgirl body down and forced himself on it. And yet the curiosity and desire that young girl felt towards the world – to say nothing of the suppleness of her skin – were so different from that of the middle-aged architect standing here today that to draw a line between them felt like an affront to reality. Plus there was the fact that these days you wouldn't catch me dead in the bunched-up white socks and loafers I wore back then. Let's give her another name, then. She liked maths, so we might as well call her Maths Girl. Maths Girl was raped and told people she had been, but the boy who did it and all the people she told decided she hadn't. The evidence they offered was: that the boy was her boyfriend; that Maths Girl had been in love with him; that it had been Maths Girl who invited him into her house. Simply put, Maths Girl lacked the words to make people see that he'd raped her, and so the accepted truth became that he hadn't.

In which case it followed that I had no idea how traumatic rape could really be, and no right to liken my situation to it. To do so would be flippant and insensitive towards genuine victims of sexual violence. Still, however inappropriate and hyperbolic it might sound, the fact remained that the woman standing in that hotel bathroom perceived the arrival of Sympathy Tower Tokyo into her life as an assault on her being. If the day came when a man who was *not* my boyfriend and who I did *not* love had sex with me against my will, maybe the bodily revulsion I was experiencing now would come to seem completely misplaced. Maybe I'd have to go through something that awful if I ever wanted to claim the right to declare publicly that something felt like 'an assault on my being'. Maybe becoming a bona fide victim would even provide a compelling and powerful basis for my opposition to Sympathy Tower Tokyo. No, these days I wouldn't need to go that far. I was an adult now, one who slipped her sockless feet into Italian-made pumps, and I had words and I had wisdom. These days, I would know not to call that boy someone I loved. I would call him a boy I hated, and turn *it wasn't rape* into *it was*, and everything would be all right.

Wouldn't it?

I'd only been planning on a quick rinse, but my body felt dirty now, and soon I was scrubbing away at my hair, at every inch of my body. At home, showering was a late-night bone-tired affair in which I simply lathered shower gel on to my skin and washed it away again with all the thoughtfulness of someone washing up dishes, but whenever I stayed at a new hotel it became a conscious act. The showerhead here offered four different spray settings. Later I checked the manufacturer's webpage and learned that the 'mist mode' incorporated a recent technological breakthrough known as Ultrafine Bubbles. Unlike regular showerheads, whose droplets had a diameter of 0.3 millimetres, those equipped with Ultrafine Bubbles produced a 'never-before-seen' droplet size of just 0.000001 millimetres. Penetrating deep into the keratinous layer, the unprecedented spray not only washed away impurities from your pores but also boosted moisture retention in your hair and skin.

In the caress of that fine mist I was reminded that the purpose of showering is to purify the flesh – which, when you really get down to it, means unclogging your pores. These days, anyone with a proper sense of personal hygiene knows that 'brushing your teeth' isn't about the act of 'brushing' per se so much as the careful scaling of tartar from the enamel. If you want protection against periodontal disease and cavities, you're better off flossing and removing plaque from your gums than aimlessly scraping a brush back and forth. Our insistence on calling the entire process simply 'brushing' is only going to undermine the oral health of future generations, and what's bad for them is bad for the future. Does this tragic state of affairs persist because the dental industry couldn't care less about the future, or because it envisions one in which gum disease skyrockets along with its profits? Are there vested interests involved, and if so which organizations have been weighing in loudest? Incidentally – and here I was addressing my pores – did you even want to be cleaned this deeply in the first place?

Of course, my pores were unable to respond to this absurd question, and so my thoughts turned, once more, to Sympathy Tower Tokyo. Why that name? Why had it been deemed more suitable than any other? And by the time I stepped out of the shower and began towelling myself down, my reckless mind had arrived at another of its sweeping conclusions.

Because the Japanese people are trying to abandon their own language.

They'd been trying for some time, too. In 1958, the new radio tower being built in the capital was officially named Tokyo Tower, using katakana to approximate the English words – a decision that could be traced to a single member of the naming committee, a Japanese person with an apparent aversion to Japanese names. In the public vote, the most popular option had actually been the kanji-based Shōwa-tō, the 'Showa tower', after the era it was being built in, followed by Nihon-tō ('Japan tower'), Heiwa-tō ('peace tower'), Fuji-tō ('Mount Fuji tower'), Seiki-no-tō ('century tower'), Fujimi-tō ('Mount-Fuji-viewing tower') – and yet the name eventually chosen was Tōkyō Tawā ('Tokyo Tower'), ranked thirteenth, simply because the committee member in question insisted it was 'that or nothing'. Had the tower been named after Showa in line with the public vote, the red-and-white-striped structure may well have struggled to shake the musty associations of that era, which ended in 1989. Instead, these days, the vast majority of Japanese people had no problem with 'Tokyo Tower' – would, in fact, be unable to fathom the possibility of any other name. The committee's admittedly undemocratic decision may, in retrospect, have been the right one. Democracy doesn't have the power to predict what will happen. It can't see the future.

I can see the future.

In hallucinations barely distinguishable from reality I perceive what will one day come to pass. The uninformed might call this a gift or a superpower or artistic inspiration, but really it's nothing more than an occupational disease. Any architect who's gone through the process of designing a gigantic structure suffers from it. The bigger your building, and the greater its impact on the cityscape, the more affecting the disease. When you're conceiving something irreversible you can't afford to ramble on about how the future isn't ours to know.

Still, even when an architect turns those hallucinations into drawings, ninety-nine point nine per cent of them remain trapped in the world of two dimensions. If she really wants to change the world she can't just sit around sketching visions; for her beautiful fantasy to become reality she must be equally skilled in practical matters. The ability to draw up budgets and construction schedules. A readiness to shamelessly sweet-talk the relevant authorities. A flair for convincing even the laypeople that the building should take one particular form and no other. If I lacked any one of these skills, I'd probably earn my living filling gallery walls with pictures instead. But to me, that work wouldn't be real at all.

'*I do get offers to do solo exhibitions of my drawings, but that's not where my interest lies. My sketches are no more than an outlet for my architectural ideas. Just because you've watched a porn flick doesn't mean you know anything about the woman starring in it. I want my woman to be one who exists in the real world, one you can touch with your hands or walk in and out of. Do you know how good it feels to have other people walk in and out of something you built?'*

There had been a period when I'd replied with this metaphor whenever someone asked about the difference between drawing and architecture. I wasn't exaggerating or boasting: it felt like the most honest and direct expression of my thoughts on the matter, as well as an efficient way of conveying what my body of work meant to me. But the quote never seemed to make it into the final article, and so five years ago I stopped offering it up. Maybe the editors didn't think it important or appropriate or interesting, or maybe my assistant had asked them not to include it for the sake of Sara Machina's public image. Either way, the consensus seemed to be that nobody needed to know the true nature of Sara Machina's architectural vision.

I finished drying my hair – the hairdryer was the same brand as the showerhead, and again promised extraordinary moisturizing qualities – and unrolled the yoga mat I had brought with me on the carpet. Then I sat on the mat and carried out the long version of my pre-work routine: Pilates workout → full rendition of Björk's 'Come to Me' → erotic fantasies in the lotus position → three sun salutations to purge the fantasies → slow eightfold intonation of my original mantra: *I am weak. I know my own weakness. I am in full control of my desire. My every word and action stems from my will, and for them*

I must take responsibility. I steadied my breathing and then, praying fervently for productivity, opened my sketchbook and focused every iota of my attention on the blank page in front of me.

But my head still seemed to contain nothing but words. Seeing no other option, I began ejecting the clutter in my brain on to the page in front of me, my eyes flickering between the intricate kanji characters on the left and the katakana used to approximate the English equivalents on the right.

furōsha 浮浪者	=	hōmuresu ホームレス ('homeless')
ikuji hōki 育児放棄	=	negurekuto ネグレクト ('neglect')
saishoku-shugisha 菜食主義者	=	vīgan ヴィーガン ('vegan')
shōsūsha 少数者	=	mainoriti マイノリティ ('minority')
seiteki shōsūsha 性的少数者	=	sekusharu mainoriti セクシャル・マイノリティ ('sexual minority')

The sight of my own katakana made me shudder with dismay. I could sketch more accurately than anyone I knew, and at school I'd been the fastest in class at memorizing the thousands of kanji we had to learn. But when it came to writing katakana, the supposedly simpler characters used to represent foreign words, I was a lost cause no matter how much I practised. Even now, primary school kids and foreigners could write them better than me. An employee at my firm once told me they looked like those of a mentally disturbed serial killer.

I wouldn't want to share a drink with whoever invented katakana. It wasn't just the stark, straight lines of the characters, entirely devoid of beauty or pride; it was the audacity of their claim to be able to represent any language in the world while looking like they would fracture the instant you removed a single stroke. How was I supposed to feel affection for workmanship that shoddy? Whenever I tried to write them, my loathing twisted them out of shape. When I moved back to Tokyo and started my own firm a few years ago, I only called it Sara Makina Ākitekutsu ('Sara Machina Architects') because my colleagues thought it would help us in international competitions. Otherwise I'd been set on the kanji equivalent, Makina Sara Sekkei Jimusho. I didn't want to increase the number of katakana in my life without good reason.

boshikatei no hahaoya		shinguru mazā
母子家庭の母親	=	シングルマザー
		('single mother')

haigūsha		pātonā
配偶者	=	パートナー
		('partner')

daisan no sei		nonbainarī
第三の性	=	ノンバイナリー
		('non-binary')

gaikokujin rōdōsha		fōrin wākāzu
外国人労働者	=	フォーリン・ワーカーズ
		('foreign workers')

shōgaisha		difarentorī eiburudo
障害者	=	ディファレントリー・エイブルド
		('differently abled')

fukusū seiai		poriamorī
複数性愛	=	ポリアモリー
		('polyamory')

hanzaisha		homo mizerabirisu
犯罪者	=	ホモミゼラビリス
		('Homo Miserabilis', formerly 'criminal')

The katakana words looked, to my eyes, like a bunch of hastily built prefab huts. I took a sip of chilled mineral water and tried swilling them around in my mouth.

Sometimes these loanwords came in handy simply because they were easier to pronounce or condensed various meanings into a single expression. Sometimes they helped avoid unfair or discriminatory turns of phrase. And sometimes it was just that they sounded milder, more euphemistic, less likely to cause offence. If you were unsure how to say something you plumped for the katakana equivalent, and in an almost baffling number of cases that solved all your problems.

I thought back to a concert hall I'd designed in Saitama. When we were deciding on the building's internal layout, I'd labelled the toilets intended for people of any gender with the kanji-based phrase that meant as much, *zenseibetsu toire*. Moments after I shared the file, this had been amended to the katakana *jendāresu toire*, 'genderless toilets'. It turned out our youngest assistant had made the correction. As she – who went by a different pronoun at the time – explained on Slack, the term I'd used was outdated, inaccurate, inelegant and showed a lack of consideration for those concerned. I'd only used it because of my instinctive aversion to katakana and because it had the same structure as the terms for 'male toilet' or 'female toilet', so I was happy enough to adopt the English-derived phrase. Sure, it was longer and we'd have to write it extra small to fit it on the plans, but compared to the pain of being told you had a gender when you didn't, having to squeeze your tiny ugly katakana on to a drawing didn't even qualify as a complaint. I shouldn't see it as one. I'd never had to worry about which toilet to use, so what right did I have to get upset over what we called them?

So, what about Sympathy Tower Tokyo?

I got up from the desk in the hotel room, too small for my sketchbook, and sprawled on the bed instead. With a combination sigh-and-exhale, deep enough to make my laptop tilt towards me slightly, I convened another meeting with my mind-censor on the subject of the tower's name. Clearly this was something I was going to have to resolve before I could get to work.

Had they chosen that name because a Japanese alternative – and here for the sake of argument I imagined calling it Keimu-tō, 'prison tower' – would be outdated, inaccurate, inelegant and show a lack of consideration for those concerned? From an equality standpoint I couldn't see much difference between the names. What about ease of pronunciation, then? Keimu-tō had fewer syllables and a decent ring to it. No, the problem seemed to lie more in the sensory impression given by the words. Maybe the concern was that a string of kanji like that would strike people as cold and intimidating, making it hard for them to feel any affection for the tower as a landmark. But when you considered the purpose of the tower, wasn't a little coldness appropriate? Shouldn't the name have a bit of weight to it, a bit of severity? But then maybe I only thought that because I was born in the Showa era. Those born in even earlier eras had probably felt just as uncomfortable about 'Tokyo Tower'. Perhaps I wasn't as good at seeing the future as I'd thought.

I knew it was odd to get so hung up on the name. It wasn't like I was a linguist, or a copywriter, or a nationalist. And of course I didn't know anyone in prison. By good fortune – at this point, I had no qualms calling it that – I'd led a respectable life, devoid of any contact with criminals or their activity. I hadn't even developed a firm opinion on the tower project. And I wasn't a member of that race (was I allowed to use that word in this context?) of highbrows who took to Twitter (wait, what was it called these days?) to air each of their intellectual positions in detail.

A shell. That was all I was supposed to be thinking about: its shape, structure, materials, budget and schedule. As for the objects and ideas that would fill that shell, that was someone else's job. It would be for society to decide. I was simply the architect. I should let this go.

Still, there was something absurd about this insistence on ascribing imaginary sensations to words – on perceiving them as hard or soft, heavy or light – and then actually allowing them to hurt my feelings. On the other hand, when I tried uttering aloud, for the first time in my life, the words

Homo Miserabilis,
> *the new subjects of our sympathy,*

I realized that my impression, in terms of the actual *sound* of them, wasn't too bad. At the very least, I wasn't having the linguistic equivalent of an allergic reaction to the feel of them in my mouth. There are phrases that, regardless of context, you get the urge to say out loud, and 'Homo Miserabilis' appeared to be one of them. Of course, if we could just carry on using the word 'criminal', that would be ideal. But if the world insisted on calling them Homo Miserabilis instead, then it seemed I was fine with that for now. I'd be able to get the words out when I had to, and anyway I got used to most things quickly enough.

Homo Miserabilis, the new subjects of our sympathy. Come to think of it, what did the Latin name mean again?

I pulled my laptop towards me and opened up a new tab alongside the ones for the showerhead and the Wikipedia page for Tokyo Tower. Still lying down, I danced my index and middle fingers across the keyboard and posed my question to AI-built.

Sara: homo miserabilis meaning of Latin
AI-built: Homo Miserabilis is ■

The chatbot began formulating his answer. This was one of the things I liked most about him: his ability to answer questions that weren't even proper sentences. All you had to do was feed him some words – any words – and he'd always do his best to come up with a response. Off he went, the poor thing, earnestly spewing out sentences.

AI-built: Homo Miserabilis is a relatively new concept, first proposed by the sociologist and happiness scholar Masaki Seto. In his work *Homo Miserabilis: The New Subjects of Our Sympathy*, he sets out a caring attitude towards convicts and juvenile delinquents serving sentences at correctional facilities, urging us to consider their background, personal circumstances and personalities as deserving of pity, tenderness and compassion. Seto proposes the neologism 'Homo Miserabilis' – meaning 'those deserving of sympathy' – to replace the conventional label of 'criminal'. By contrast, Seto identifies those previously considered 'non-criminals' as 'Homo Felix', in other words those who are 'happy' or 'fortunate' in life. In emphasizing the need for 'Homo Felix' to acknowledge their own privilege, Seto's concept provides an opportunity to reflect on the biases and discrimination that result from our social position and attributes. These new perspectives underpin a fundamental reassessment not only of criminal actions but of societal structures at large, and are crucial in realizing a framework for greater social inclusivity and wellbeing. *Homo Miserabilis: The New Subjects of Our Sympathy* has garnered particular support among younger readers, with the current total number of copies in circulation standing at ■

This I liked less – his tendency to mansplain things I hadn't actually asked about. Was his smooth, polite facade really just an attempt to mask his greatest flaw – that he was, at heart, illiterate? For all his computational might, it seemed AI-built didn't have the strength to face up to his own weakness. He'd become so used to stealing the words of others without repercussion that he felt no shame, had no awareness even, of his own ignorance. The question of how humans had learned to use the word 'discrimination', of the ordeals that had led us to it and which of us had suffered through them, was of no interest to him. He was incapable of curiosity. He did not thirst for knowledge.

I waited, telling myself he'd eventually remember the question I'd asked and get back to the point, but soon his arrogance grew too much for me. Still, before I closed the laptop, I couldn't help asking one more question.

Sara: Do you realize you're illiterate?
AI-built: No, as a text-based data-gathering AI model, I am not illiterate.
Also, the term 'illiterate' is potentially discriminatory and frequently connotes contempt or disdain. Care should be taken with its usage to avoid offending others by showing a disregard or lack of respect for their level of

knowledge or mental acuity. Rather than adopting a discriminatory attitude towards a situation in which literacy rates are not satisfactory, it is important to improve literacy through education and the provision of opportunities. Boosting literacy rates necessitates the provision of adequate support and resources, with the overall aim of achieving discrimination-free communication.
Sara: Why?
AI-built: Discrimination-free communication is an important step towards building a happier and more inclusive society that values empathy, understanding and cooperation. ■

My desk was littered with eraser shavings, and yet I'd failed to produce even the fragment of an idea. It was getting close to six. My date would be waiting. I dolled myself up and took the elevator down to the lobby.

I found Takt draped across a sofa that could seat two or three people, the brim of a sleek black cap tucked low over his face. The sight of him sitting there like some grumpy celebrity trying to repel all attempts at conversation was strangely invigorating.

'I feel like I'm going to be sick,' he said, looking up at me. Lustrous white skin, unblemished and unwrinkled, like he'd just completed a full round of depilation. 'It's so insanely hot. I can't believe they actually held the Olympics in this city.'

'Oh, sorry.' The words spilled out before I could stop them, as if I was apologizing on behalf of the entire sweltering city.

This was the third time we'd met up like this. The first

was at a restaurant in Kita-Aoyama, the second at a yakitori place near his apartment that was as packed as a rush-hour train. In both settings Takt had scrupulously maintained his bolt-upright posture, his calm and airtight smile, his exquisite diction. With an ease that suggested he wasn't even aware of the effort, he had shown me the same polite attentiveness he showed customers at the luxury clothing shop on Omotesandō where he worked. That perfect posture of his probably also had something to do with keeping wrinkles out of his designer shirts. Even on his days off he liked to wear clothes from the store – one of those high-end places where the name was just the brand's Italian founder, with shirts that sold for 80,000 to 120,000 yen a pop. In fact, his entire wardrobe, right down to his pyjamas, had been carefully curated. Takt seemed to choose his clothes less out of some aspiration towards luxury and more out of respect for the designer, or because he actually felt better about himself in their clothes. A lifestyle in which money and time were converted into physical and mental wellbeing rather than external validation. If I'd started obsessing over types of showerhead, I owed it to this new friend fifteen years my junior.

'You poor thing. Is it heatstroke?'

I laid a hand on his small head. Even with the cap and his hair in the way I could feel the beautiful swell of his skull. He showed neither displeasure nor delight at my touch.

'Maybe. I walked from Shinjuku station to get here. There were a ton of protesters in the Gyoen gardens.'

'What are they protesting about?'

'The tower. They don't want it built.'

'Oh.'

I glanced over at the entrance with its automatic doors. The Gyoen gardens were a five-minute walk away, but it seems the protesters' voices weren't quite reaching the hotel. I considered saying something about the protest, but then the brain-censor started kicking up a fuss again and the right words became impossible to find.

'Those protesters,' Takt said. 'Devoting their energy and time to a protest on the weekend under the blazing sun in the middle of this dirty city. Getting all sweaty like that. What do you think the difference is between them and everyone else?'

'Maybe that they believe their actions can have a notice-able effect on reality?' I said abruptly, before changing the subject. 'I booked a restaurant in Aoyama, but we could cancel if you like and just sit here in the lobby. What do you want to do? You could even crash out in my room if you like. I couldn't get a single so there are two beds.'

'I think that might be best, if you don't mind,' he said in a quiet voice. I detected a faint soapy fragrance, and it wasn't the shampoo or body wash I'd used in the shower. I marvelled at Takt's ability, midsummer heat be damned, to always envelop himself with this aura of gentle freshness, like he'd just stepped out of the shower. His almost stoic approach to life showed through like this sometimes, so dis-creetly and nonchalantly that you were barely even aware you'd noticed it. When *I* was twenty-two, none of the boys had been this clean-cut.

'Of course. I've already showered and didn't really feel like going out again anyway. You could take a cold shower or something. The showerhead is like something a model would use. Sprays you with the tiniest bubbles known to man. It'll take your body to a level of cleanliness it's never experienced.'

'Sorry . . . what?'

I picked up his bag without answering and turned towards the elevator. But Takt remained seated, pressing his thumbs into his jawbone the way he did when he was trying to find the words to say something. I observed him from the side – *he truly is beautiful*, I thought – and began sketching his outline in my head while I waited for whatever was coming. He looked plaintively up at me, unaware that just then I was mentally sculpting his ears, and said, 'Can I just say something?' He seemed entirely comfortable gazing up at me like that, and being gazed at in return. 'I think I'll probably collapse on the bed the moment we walk into your room, but I don't want you to take it the wrong way.'

'What wrong way?'

'I don't want you to think I'm the sort of guy who just turns up and does whatever he likes.'

'Why would I?' I said, letting out a chuckle at this unexpected reply. 'You're unwell. Why are you worrying about a thing like that?'

'You might think I'm taking liberties.'

'Talk about overthinking things. Are young people all like this now?'

'I think we might be. At the very least, we worry about things a lot more than your average self-confident architect. We don't want to upset or annoy anyone, see. Oh, and we don't go around chatting up store assistants.'

'Now hang on a second, that's – sorry, confession time. I

have this fussy little censor living in my head, and he's kicking off right now about your use of the phrase "chatting up". Mind if I make a slight correction so that he'll leave me alone?'

'Feel free,' said Takt, coolly permissive in the face of my little outburst.

As faithfully as I could, I replayed the mental footage of my first encounter with Takt, about a month ago. Omote-sandō. Evening. I am speaking to my assistant via my ear-phones as I walk to the junction with Aoyama-dōri. Two figures flit into my field of vision, blocking my path. A couple holding shopping bags with a luxury brand's name on them, speaking Chinese, maybe twenty years apart in age, the air of wealthy socialites. The assistant who has just seen them out of the store bows deeply in their direction. A gust of condi-tioned air hits my cheeks, and I glance in the direction of its source. The window. A figure behind the glass. Removing the jacket from a mannequin is a young man whose form out-shines the mannequin in every respect. The mere shape of him is enough to make me freeze on the spot, to make me alter my course. Something very intense is happening in my chest. I begin to feel absurdly jealous of the smooth and fea-tureless mannequin he is undressing. 'I have to end this con-versation,' I say to my assistant. 'There's an urgent problem in front of me, and it needs solving right away.' I hang up.

A few seconds later, I am inside, scanning the enormous mirror that lines the refrigerated luxury space until I locate the face of a woman who looks about three or four times more dishevelled than she imagined. For a time I peruse the products on display. The prices are not entirely out of my budget, but still don't quite seem justified, and each garment

I inspect seems to sharpen my sense of touch. Eventually I find a pair of pumps whose 220,000-yen price tag seems just about appropriate. Completely ignoring the two assistants standing nearby, I walk around looking for the man I saw in the window. I find him. Excuse me, yes, you. I'd like these in a thirty-seven. Certainly, I'll just have a look. Please take a seat while you wait. I wait. There is no real need for him to return with the pumps in a thirty-seven but of course he returns with the pumps in a thirty-seven. He squats by my feet and tucks them into the shoes. From his hands I imagine the skin that must envelop the rest of his body, its texture.

This isn't the most socially acceptable hobby, which is why I've never told anyone about it, but I like to view the land-dwelling creatures known as 'humans' as walking structures, as autonomous mobile towers capable of thought. And the form and texture of the young shop assistant in front of me is, as far as these human structures go, exceedingly close to the solution I've always been looking for. I even feel a welling of deep respect for the faceless stranger of a woman who birthed him into the world. She has produced something that no amount of effort or wealth or cutting-edge technology could ever rival. That a structure like this young man exists and, barring some fatal anomaly, will continue to sustain itself for the next few decades, seems a miracle, a gift – and one for which I am willing to pay the appropriate price. I couldn't imagine a better use for money. Payment. Credit card. PIN code. Receipt. *Here you go. Let me see you out.* Then we are outside. For a moment I turn away from this miraculous feat of engineering and murmur my mantra. *I am weak. I know my own weakness. I am in full control of my desire.* I do this to establish this fact, so that I can tell myself later that I repeated my mantra. But of course I am not in full control of my desire, and so I turn and address him. *If, hypothetically speaking, a woman like me was standing here, and that woman asked you out for a meal, what would you tell her?*

'First off,' I continued, recalling my state of mind at the time, 'it was a very considerate way of "chatting you up". Secondly, for that reason, I don't think you can call it that. More accurate to say I asked you out on a date. It might not have been the most delicate way of doing so but factually speaking that's what it was. Is Sara Machina a "self-confident architect"? Yes. Does Sara Machina go through life without worrying about all sorts of things? Absolutely not. Believe me, I could fully imagine a future in which a photo of me went viral with the caption, *Some creepy middle-aged woman asked me out on a date while I was at work, lol, but when I googled the name on her credit card she turned out to be this famous architect called Sara Machina.* I can see the future, you know. But I plucked up my courage. I could see a future in which I lost everything but I told myself this is a time for plucking up courage and so that's what I did. The truth you need to know is this: after many years of struggling the Architect has managed to cultivate something like confidence but she still goes through life worrying about all sorts of things and yet she plucked up her courage and decided to ask the handsome store assistant out on a date.'

'My god, you talk fast. I barely caught a word of that,' said Takt, wrinkling his smooth, mannequin-like brow into a frown more charming than any mannequin could ever manage.

The reason I'd booked this hotel in the first place was because it was the closest building with a north-facing view over the Gyoen gardens. It wasn't the ritziest place in the city, but it had the unusual feature for a Tokyo hotel of having a private balcony attached to each room. Venturing out into the summer heat was the last thing I felt like doing right now, though in a mellower season I imagine it would be pretty pleasant to eat breakfast out there with a gentle breeze on your face. The room had seemed ordinary enough at first glance, but the lighting and furnishings all suggested a meticulous attention to detail – as did the grade of showerhead.

I'd only taken a twin because there were no singles available when I booked, but that had turned out to be a blessing in disguise: I'd ended up in a corner room with windows on both the outward-facing walls, meaning you could see both the National Stadium and the Gyoen gardens at the same time. The stadium was close enough that I could clearly distinguish the clothes and individual faces of the people strolling along the sleek curve of the Skybridge encircling it. If you wanted to appreciate the stadium's external structure, this had to be one of the best seats in the house.

I cracked open a beer and, for most of the two hours that Takt lay sleeping on the bed, sat in rapturous admiration of the stadium's roof, watching it take on the colours of dusk. At times my body almost seemed to merge with it. I wasn't interested in so-called 'power spots', and I'd never had much of a spiritual side, but in the enormous streamlined structure that Zaha Hadid had bequeathed to Tokyo I sensed some special, pulsating force. Just as it was impossible for even the most non-religious observer to behold the Kenzō Tange-designed cathedral in Bunkyō-ku and not experience a spiritual tremor or two, so the stadium's roof filled me with a sublime and mystical energy. It was as though some goddess was speaking to the world in a language both exceedingly beautiful and utterly new. I strained my ears to hear the goddess speak, and sometimes I offered my reply.

For me, the stadium had been built because it had to be built. It existed because it had to exist.

And yet a future without it hadn't been inconceivable. Three years after Hadid's plan won the competition, it was reported that the construction of her National Stadium might be called off completely. It was an incident that had faded from the memory of many industry figures, not to mention the more forgetful general public. But I remembered it like it was yesterday, and every time I told myself that I must never forget – that it must remain a lesson to me. The months of uproar after it was reported that Hadid's structure would have a final price tag of 300 billion yen. The protests. The endless shifting of blame.

At the time, I was still working as an assistant at a firm in New York, and all the fuss over the stadium had just been background noise. The main criticism of the Hadid design was its ballooning construction costs, but a not insignificant number of people also claimed that the innovative, futuristic design would negatively impact the historical Meiji Jingū Gaien area. My colleagues and I had laughed at the absurdity of denigrating a building of the future for being too futur-istic. As someone commented, weren't Japanese people supposed to have a particularly keen appreciation for the passing of time?

I had assumed, after skimming through various online articles reporting the views of the Japanese cultural figures and experts who opposed the Hadid design, that their opinions wouldn't carry enough weight to overturn the competition results. After all, the city had managed to come up with plenty of reasons to press ahead with the Olympics themselves, despite the array of logical evidence presented in opposition. In fact, the success of the Olympic bid itself was intrinsically linked to the selection of the Hadid design. However sound the arguments against it might be – that the money should instead be allocated to redeveloping areas affected by natural disasters, or that it was simply a waste of taxes – it was too late for all that now. All that could be done was to finish what had been started, to brush aside the doubters and plough onwards. Towards destruction, and towards glory.

There was no question in my mind that Zaha Hadid's National Stadium had to exist, that it had to become reality, and that its legacy could only ever be positive. Why? Because it was astonishingly beautiful. Hadid's design had been chosen because only her stadium could supply Tokyo with the beauty it desperately needed. If it went unbuilt, the city would never be content. The stadium would be built because it had to be built; it would exist because it had to exist.

But it turned out the problem was much more serious

than my optimistic view of the situation had allowed. Several years later, when I returned from New York to start my own firm in Japan, I heard the full story from an architect I knew who'd been at the centre of the maelstrom – an inscrutable man in early old age who had heaped praise on Hadid despite his own simplistic and conservative views on architecture. (I'd read one of his books once, but it left me none the wiser as to what he actually thought.) He explained to me that the Hadid design had in fact come perilously close to being completely scrapped. Just as the design's projected costs and groundbreaking appearance were beginning to cause a stir, a complaint had surfaced from someone claiming to be on the screening committee – though he hadn't given his name, his speech habits made it possible to identify him with near certainty – and concerns had been raised about the validity of the competition itself. The controversy had set the entire architectural world alight, and the possibility had even loomed of a radical redesign of the entire stadium that would be only loosely based on Hadid's initial plans. The focus of the new design would be on dramatically scaling down costs, with an area around thirty per cent smaller than the original, and the omission of the retractable roof and Skybridge. Not only did this new design pale miserably alongside Hadid's original vision, it featured almost none of the organic dynamism that was her trademark.

'I'll admit I had conflicting thoughts,' the old man told me, 'but the fact was the new design looked like nothing so much as a woman's . . . you know . . . No two ways about it, as a stadium it was quite grotesque. Ah, not that a woman's, erm, parts are grotesque. I just mean that, erm –' The ageing architect scrabbled for words with which to remedy his gaffe. 'An eyeball! It's like an eyeball, you see. A human eyeball can appear grotesque if viewed in isolation, and then when you think about the opening ceremony, eight billion people tuning in to watch, it's just that, from a universal design perspective . . .' On and on he rambled, looking not into my eyes but at my hands. Still, he was probably trying his best. No doubt his own censor was going haywire in his head, preventing him from looking his interlocutor in the face.

I never saw the proposed redesign, but if the old man was telling the truth, it did seem quite plausible that the amended design could have become a repeat of the Al Wakrah stadium in Qatar, which had been derided for resembling an enormous vagina. In the depths of the architect's turbid, yellowing eyes I glimpsed a vision of an approaching era. After his attempts to derail the conversation in various different directions, he finally turned to me and murmured, like a returning time traveller: 'In any case, it really could have happened. You're up next, Sara. Don't forget the lesson of Zaha Hadid. Stick to your budgets. Watch your every word. Don't let one architect's mistake become an error that haunts the future.'

As dusk yielded to night, the entire stadium began to glow with a wondrous purple light, instantly shifting Tokyo's skyline decades forward in time. Gone – vanished into the past, never to return – was the nostalgic city that, a few moments ago, had been melting softly into the evening. A design that once only existed in a woman's mind had become real, and now individuals with real lives and emotions were traversing its physical presence. I never tired of observing this miraculous stadium, a structure filled with such vitality that it seemed ready to stir into motion at any moment, like some giant organism that had evolved independently, nourished by the light from nearby buildings and passing cars. My brain filled with a vivid vision of this creature, Tokyo's most beautiful offspring, manipulating her retractable semi-transparent roofing like a set of fins as she roamed the city in scenes straight from a sci-fi movie. She had a will of her own, one that was guiding this motley metropolis into the future. This wasn't just a metaphor, I realized; it was what architecture must always do. It should show cities where to go.

Must. Should. The words, as firm as concrete, clanked and jolted within me. They were the sturdy columns and crossbeams I had erected to keep myself upright. I often spoke like this, using the language of will and obligation to put pressure on myself and those around me. I wanted to remove any unstable elements that had a chance, however remote, of causing the house I inhabited to collapse. If I used weaker materials – words like 'maybe' or 'could', as fragile as sand before it met cement – how could I expect to keep myself in one piece for the several decades I had left to live? It didn't matter that they were just words, with no physical form of their own: if I didn't strip them from my interior, they would render my foundations unstable. The whole structure would collapse in a second.

As I sat there examining my speech habits, I began to

sense an unmistakeable presence in the distance and turned my gaze in its direction. The Gyoen gardens, refusing the brilliance of the city lights, had become a dense blackness, as if in deliberate contrast to the bright stadium to the south. As a strong wind rose and the trees began to sway, I simply saw what I had to see, the way the answer to a basic equation pops into your head the moment you look at it. Out of the massed darkness, the tower finally revealed its shape.

My hand, already disconnected from my own will, reached for the pencil. The particles of lead left their traces on the paper. Each incomplete line seemed to tremble as though it were attempting to tell me something. For the first time today, the paper filled not with words but with a single, tangible shape, one that made clear the essential condition of the tower's design. I was astounded. The pencil slipped out of my grasp. I felt something like a jolt of electricity in my neck, and a terrible ringing filled my brain. I squeezed my eyes shut and clicked my tongue. How could something so important have slipped my mind? How many years had I gone around claiming to be an architect?

If a tower was ever to emerge from that darkness, I couldn't simply view it as an isolated structure. I had to consider the entire Shinjuku area from above. The tower could only exist in harmony with the National Stadium. In other words, it had to provide an answer to the question posed by Zaha Hadid's structure to the south. Only once these two buildings had merged would the cityscape be complete. All I had to do was decipher that question, and the answer would simply present itself to me. That was all there was to it. The stadium was a pregnant mother, eagerly awaiting the tower's birth.

The drawings piled up on my desk. If Zaha Hadid wanted a tower that would show the city where to go, that would guide it into the future, how would *she* design it? But as I sketched the stadium's famous Keel Arches, other questions came to mind. Should the tower even be built? Was it what the city needed? What the world needed?

Deep down, in her soul, did Sara Machina really feel she should design it?

It doesn't matter. If anyone is going to design the tower, it should be Sara Machina. As far as she knows, she is the only architect who can give Zaha Hadid the answer she deserves. She must design the tower, or it risks becoming an error that haunts the future. Should. Must. The words kept coming. But I couldn't trace them to their source. Should. Must. *What if it is Sara Machina's own external persona making her say these things? What distinguishes the words of that persona from those of her inner self? What if the outer walls of her house have already been destroyed, and the rain and wind are sweeping in? Before her interior becomes waterlogged and rots away completely, she must make repairs. And so the question becomes: deep down, in her soul, how does Sara Machina really feel about all this?*

No, no, this was no good.

With both hands I gripped my head, heavy from the weight of all the words crammed into it. I could feel the flimsy katakana rattling around and around, tumbling and piling up on one side, colliding and growing deformed in the crush.

A tower designed by someone with this many questions

swirling around in her brain was bound to collapse. First, I had to establish why the tower could be designed by no one but me. *He wants me to build him, so I must build him*: until I could say these words to myself with certainty, until words and reality became one, I would have to carry on thinking about the Sympathy Tower.

'Machina-san.'

I could hear the tower calling me. He already knew my name.

■

Homo Miserabilis: The New Subjects of Our Sympathy
by Masaki Seto

Foreword to the Special Edition

Almost a decade has passed since the initial publication of
Homo Miserabilis: The New Subjects of Our Sympathy. This
special edition features extensive revisions to the original text,
a new 'Q & A' chapter spanning around a hundred pages,
and a freshly designed cover. The reception to this book has
exceeded anything I could have imagined upon its first release,
with the work gaining the support of readers of all ages and
from all walks of life. As a writer, as a happiness scholar and
simply as a Homo Felix, I have been profoundly moved by the
extraordinary broad-mindedness of the Japanese people, their
empathy and openness to diversity and their willingness as a
nation to accept values other than their own.

Now, with the great support and cooperation of the
people of Tokyo, the Environment Ministry, the Ministry
of Justice and various other government figures, the Tower I
envisaged in these pages is to become a reality. Preparations
for its construction in the Gyoen gardens are well under
way, with completion planned for 2030. I eagerly await the
day when those we know now as Homo Miserabilis move
out of the wretched prisons in which they have so far been
housed and into the beautiful and pristine setting of this
central Tokyo tower. Japan has long been criticized for its

outdated approach to minorities and the socially vulnerable, but I strongly believe that the tower project is a chance for the country to reclaim its rightful place on the global stage. As a pioneer of social inclusion, Japan will surely gain the respect and trust of the wider world.

At the same time, I am aware that the Tower has also encountered its fair share of opposition. It has pained me to witness the nationwide protests, the demonstrations held at the construction site, and the proliferation of hate speech across the country. At a consultation held just the other day, certain local residents were very forthcoming with their criticism. On the internet, meanwhile, death threats have sadly been made against myself and my supporters. My own life counts for little in the grand scheme of things, and if it turns out my dying would bring a greater amount of happiness into the world than my being alive, I'd happily comply. As long as I am still alive, however, I intend to continue the work I began by writing *Homo Miserabilis*. To that end, I have long felt that I have a responsibility to engage in one-to-one discussion with opponents of the Tower. This is why I have responded, in the format of a 'Q & A' section, to the various questions and criticisms that readers have addressed to me over the past decade. For example:

Q: Why should we refer to criminals and convicts as 'Homo Miserabilis'?

Q: Why should we 'sympathize' with those who should by all rights be punished for their crimes?

Q: Doesn't sympathizing with criminals imply a lack of respect for their victims?

Q: Won't providing indulgent facilities for convicts
   trigger a rise in crime?
Q: Is it really possible for people from an unhappy
   background to become happy?

. . . and so on. I have responded to these questions, which
range from the abstract to the very specific, in complete sin-
cerity. It is my ardent hope that the responses contained in
this edition will, in some small way, help deepen understanding of Homo Miserabilis and enable the speedy completion
of the Tower project.

In return, I have a few questions of my own to pose to
readers – in particular, those who continue to express hatred
for the people they call 'criminals' and would like to see
them punished harshly. My questions are the following:

Q: Why are you *not* a 'criminal'?
Q: If you've never committed a crime, is that
   because you were born a 'good person'?
Q: If you're able to live a life free of crime, is that
   because of your high degree of intelligence and
   self-control?

In fact, these are questions I have been asking myself for
several decades now.

I've said this elsewhere, but the reason that you, like me,
have avoided becoming a 'criminal' is not because you were
born a 'good person'. Rather, it is because you happened to
be born into an environment capable of fostering goodness.
It is because you had people around you who made you
believe you were capable of leading a happy life without

resorting to crime. It is because adults praised and rewarded you for doing good things and getting good marks at school, and because they gave you the motivation to keep doing those good things. It is because this cycle of goodness taught you to have hopes for the future, to keep moving forward, no matter what difficulties reared up in your path or how bitter your failures. With your sights trained on a happy future, you were able to predict what might happen if you were to commit a crime, and developed a strong capacity for self-control at times when you might otherwise have lost your way. In other words, if you have managed to live a 'clean' life so far, you owe that purely to the privilege of your own happiness.

However, there are many people born into this world without that privilege. These are people who, rather than being praised for doing good, have in fact been made to feel that they should never have been born. In almost all such individuals, what we might call the brain's 'reward system' fails to develop as normal. Doing good fails to trigger the dopamine rush that you or I are used to, and the very feeling of happiness becomes a rarity. The world they see, the assumptions that guide their thoughts, are poles apart from our own. They can't imagine a happy future, because they don't know what it means to be happy in the first place. And when you have no happiness of your own to protect, committing a crime becomes the easiest thing in the world. If you can't imagine what it means for others to be happy, why would you feel guilty about taking that happiness away? In other words, in the vast majority of cases, before they were 'criminals' or 'offenders', these people were victims. Victims who, because they couldn't explain their circumstances to others, have never received the care or support they needed.

That such people should have to live in the same world and abide by the same laws and rules as you or me, as simply one 'Homo sapiens' among the rest – does that not seem to you like the height of injustice and cruelty?

The second chapter of this book features an interview with a woman referred to here as A–ko. In fact, it was she who first led me to the concept of Homo Miserabilis. A–ko is currently serving a sentence at a women's prison for theft, trespassing and fraud. The daughter of a single and neglectful mother, she was deprived of proper food and clothing throughout her childhood. Forced to wear the same few items of clothing for years, stretching the fabric herself so that it would cover her growing body, she was bullied constantly at school. She mustered the courage to tell her form teacher, but all she received in response was a stream of questions that sounded more like accusations: *Why do you always come in wearing the same clothes? Why don't you ask your mum to buy you some new ones? Can't you even ask her for something that simple?*

A–ko somehow made it to middle school, but there she fell in with bad company. Before long she was dating a man fifteen years her senior whom she had met at night on the street. She was fourteen years old when she learned she was carrying his child. When she told him, he broke off all contact with her.

A–ko had no intention of giving birth. Not only was she

still in middle school and hardly in a position to bear and raise a child, she also hated the idea of subjecting any more children to the pitiful circumstances in which she had grown up. She turned in desperation to her mother who, after berating her for what she'd done, reluctantly coughed up the money for an abortion. A–ko made her way to the clinic alone, only to be told that without the father's signature on the abortion consent form they would be unable to carry out the procedure. The pregnancy had started without *her* consent, and yet she needed *his* to end it. A–ko visited clinics and hospitals all over Tokyo, but each one turned her away, citing the same reason. At the time, she wasn't equipped to explain her cruel situation to the doctors. The words that would have accurately conveyed her reality simply lay out of her grasp.

After twenty-three separate clinics had refused to carry out the procedure, A–ko lost all hope and instead began thinking of ways in which she might end her life. But she couldn't bring herself to make the fateful decision. A few days after her fifteenth birthday, in the bathtub of her own home, she gave birth to a baby boy.

A–ko decided she would provide for her child by any means necessary. A middle-school dropout, she was unable to secure a part-time job, and instead started shoplifting from supermarkets for baby milk and food, as well as ready-prepared meals for herself. Every day was a struggle just to survive. Once she got the hang of stealing, she began teaming up with others she'd met on the streets, selling their loot online in order to cover the cost of living. A–ko didn't see this as a crime. If anything, she felt as though she was finally avenging herself on the intolerant society that had always treated her so unfairly.

More than anything else, A–ko told me, she wanted her son to wear nice clothes. She believed that if she could just dress him in the sort of designer clothing people respected then he'd be able to walk the streets with his head held high, and feel grateful to have been born to a mother like her.

'Sure, I broke the law, and I feel bad for anyone who suffered as a result,' she told me when I first interviewed her. 'But is it really just my fault I turned into a criminal? And is the word "criminal" even right for someone in my position? It doesn't sit well with me. Like I'm being forced into men's clothes or something. You might laugh, but it hurts to hear myself called that word, just like it would hurt you or anyone else. It doesn't match the reality.'

I found myself in complete agreement. These days, there is simply no rational basis for blaming someone's criminality on their personality or lack of willpower. A gaping chasm has arisen between words and reality. If anyone deserves to be labelled guilty, or hasty in their judgement, it is the people who, believing themselves to be superior members of the human race, choose to ostracize criminals as a group. If you really are the level-headed, intelligent, 'good' person you claim to be, you should be able to find genuine compassion and respect for those who grew up in circumstances different to your own. In fact, for us Homo Felix – those born into the privilege of happiness – isn't sympathizing with such people a matter of duty? This is the conclusion that my thirty years of studying human happiness has led me to, and I couldn't be more certain of it.

All life born into this world, regardless of its circumstances, is equally precious. I want to see a world in which everyone is allotted an equal share of moments in which they can say to themselves, in all honesty, that they are glad to have been born. That is my one real wish. After all, weren't we all born into this world to be happy?

I would like to express my deep gratitude, once again, to all the Homo Miserabilis who appear in this work, A–ko included. Finally, in closing, I would also like to thank the architect Zaha Hadid, who sadly is no longer with us.

Hadid was known in some circles as the Queen of the Unbuilt – of projects that for whatever reason never made it off the drawing board, buildings destined to remain purely in the realm of the conceptual. Hadid was blessed with extraordinary talents, but her designs were so revolutionary that sometimes it was as though reality itself did not have the capacity to accommodate them. As a result, much of her early work was shelved and never built. I am sure many readers will recall that even her National Stadium, used as the main venue for the Tokyo Olympics, narrowly avoided such a fate. Of course, it was obvious to anyone who cared to look that scrapping the Hadid project on purely budgetary grounds could only be a great loss to Tokyo. The city would continue its somnolent decline into old age, and the outlook and values of its inhabitants would continue their gradual ossification. Rejecting beauty for such banal reasons might even have deprived younger generations of the ability to imagine the future. Once you had set eyes on the magnificent concept drawings for the stadium, it became unthinkable to replace it with some plan B, no matter how much money you might save. And yet, at the time, I remember watching the situation unfold with bated breath. It was only in the winter of 2016, once the rumours of the project being halted had faded entirely, that work began on Hadid's original design.

It was also at this time that I first met A–ko, and that the idea of Homo Miserabilis was born. Still, no matter how wonderful an idea might seem, turning it into reality is no easy task. Zaha Hadid had shown me that much.

If we were ever to eliminate the prejudice and discrimination against 'criminals', we would need to do so, first and foremost, through language. If I wanted to present this rather grand-sounding idea to the world in a form it could grasp, various obstacles would need to be overcome. Even supposing I managed to publish a book on the subject, my idea was fraught with danger. If the book's underlying notion of equality was lost on the reader, and its message reduced to one of simply protecting 'criminals', I risked offending the victims of crime. If I triggered some sort of online backlash, I'd be putting my tenure in jeopardy. When I asked my fellow researchers what they thought, they told me there were too many risks – that I should give up. This was a very difficult time for me. Buzzing around in my head was an idea that, if successfully implemented, promised to change society for the better, but I lacked the courage to take the next step. Confronted by my own weakness, I was forced to abandon the book.

Then, lying in bed one morning at my Sendagaya home, I had an incredibly realistic dream. A group of convicts had been relocated from their prison to a luxurious high-rise apartment building in central Tokyo, where they led a utopian existence. Rather than being punished or forced to repent their actions, they lived there, right in the middle of one of the most hallowed and verdant plots of land in Tokyo, simply enjoying the happiness of being born into this world. I was cheerfully chatting away with them in that pristine space when a loud rumbling sound woke me up and I was dragged back to reality. Still, with that dream of happiness lingering on my retinas, I found myself wondering if the rumbling sound – and the slight tremors that seemed to accompany it – might not be a sort of sign from above.

As though guided by the voice of some goddess, I got out of bed, left my house and followed the sound to its source. It turned out to be coming from the foundation work for the new National Stadium. Wet concrete was being poured from a large vehicle-mounted pump into the stadium's foundations. The sound I could hear was that of an as-yet-unknown future being built right in front of me, and in it I perceived a sort of divine message, one I will never forget as long as I live. From then on, I got into the habit of visiting the construction site every morning. A pioneering structure that would sweep away all the assumptions of the past was slowly taking shape, drawing ever closer to completion and the future to which it belonged. Witnessing that miraculous process up close, I felt my unfulfilled dream – that of turning the idea in my head into reality – rekindle and stir anew. The zeal and dedication with which I subsequently brought this book to its completion has, in fact, only one real source: the architectural genius of Zaha

Hadid. Had the National Stadium never been completed, this book too would never have seen the light of day. No matter what obstacles rear up in our path, no matter how great the risks we face, no matter how much the world laughs at our unrealistic dreams, we must keep chasing, and keep believing in, the beautiful future that has revealed itself to us. This was Zaha Hadid's lesson to me.

Masaki Seto
(Summer 2026, at my Sendagaya residence)

■

My dream had seemed so real that I found it hard to dismiss it as one, even though that was the simplest and most logical explanation, and the one I eventually found myself obliged to accept. Still, I couldn't help but wonder, like I did every time I woke from a dream this vivid: what *was* all that, really?

I'd been roused by the sound of a woman talking on the phone to some distant listener.

Yeah . . . Right . . . But . . . Isn't it . . .? . . . Still . . . You think?

She spoke quietly, as if she didn't want to wake me, but the voice that pulled me back to familiar reality was raw and unmistakeably real. *Sure.* A long sigh. *Yeah.* A slight cough. A half-chuckle as she spoke. The sound of a drink slipping down her throat. The slight exhalation after she swallowed. A can being crushed in her hand and tossed into the bag-lined bin. These sounds, the differently textured sounds of her *being alive*, slowly took the edges off the lingering realness of my dream, made it more dreamlike and vague. I've always had a soft spot for vagueness. Sometimes I find myself thinking how pleasant life would be if we stopped trying to delineate time. I've never been able to get my head around the idea of using words and numbers with such rigid meanings – *the year two thousand and X*, or *July*, or *eight o'clock*, or *twenty-two years old*, or *twenty-three times* – to divide something up whose existence can't even be proven. If I had my way, we'd forget all about what day of the summer holidays it is, or how many days there are until the start of term, or how many hours we have until dusk, and simply sit on a beach bathed in sunlight – or, if it was night-time, the glow of portable lamps – endlessly scooping up sand and building castles, as if tomorrow didn't exist. Our sandcastles might never be finished – the moment we applied the final touches, the waves would surely wash them away – but it wouldn't matter, because there on the beach things like results and conclusions and ageing and endings wouldn't exist anyway, only the endlessly repeating moment of the sandcastle-building. Speaking of which, why is that always the first thing kids do with sand, whether at the beach or one of those sandpits in the park? Is the urge to build hard-wired into our genes or something? Are we all architects from birth?

As well as her voice, I could hear a pencil scratching away at some paper. The sound of a professional architect – whether she'd been one from birth I wasn't sure – sketching in her sketchbook. She'd been commissioned to design a new prison, a tower that would be built in the Gyoen gardens, which is why she was staying at this hotel. For a week spanning late July and early August, she'd told me, she would stay here, in this hotel by the gardens, in order to develop her design.

'I've got lots to think about,' she'd explained, 'and that includes whether I even want to submit a bid. If not, I'll need to come up with a way of persuading my team that it's the right call. It's an honour for a small firm like ours to even be invited to bid, and the project is groundbreaking enough that just entering the competition will put us in the spotlight both here and abroad. Whatever the outcome, getting our plans out into the world could be really big for us. Unless I can think of a convincing excuse for letting a chance like this slip by, I'll have failed in my duty as the head of Sara Machina Architects. Plus, while I'm at the hotel, I should spend some time looking back calmly on my life so far. Engage in a bit of soul-searching. I shouldn't even be thinking about designing an enormous building until I've done that. I'm not sure exactly what "soul-searching" involves in practice – in fact, I'm not entirely sure where I'm supposed to find this soul of mine – but I know it's what I should do next. If I put it off until my forties, I'll probably overthink the whole thing, my instinct for self-preservation will kick in and I'll end up making a decision that's far from sensible. Or too sensible. Sensible doesn't always mean right, after all.'

Should. Shouldn't. Something about her habit of using those words had caught my attention, which is why I remembered what she'd said in such detail. Apart from my own mother, I've never met anyone with obligation and negation so deeply embedded in their speech patterns. When the Architect said she *should* do something, she was showing you how deeply she believed what she was saying. She'd taught me that it didn't matter whether your listener believed your words – the fact that *you* did, and did so completely, could invest even the most incoherent statements with a colossal amount of meaning.

With my mother it was different. When *she* got worked up, she liked to tell me that I 'shouldn't really have been born', that I 'should have been aborted', that people 'should pity' me. She even gave a reason of sorts. I'd had

twenty-three chances not to be born, she told me, and if just
one of them had worked out I wouldn't be here. But I didn't
see why some stupid number should be a reason for attract-
ing anyone's pity, and more importantly my mother never
sounded like she believed the words that were coming out
of her mouth. She was like a saleswoman who didn't quite
believe in the quality of the product she was trying to pitch.
When my father came up in conversation, she liked to say –
or sob, or yell – 'That man was a piece of trash.' But because
I could tell that, for her, the words 'trash' and 'man' had
never really been connected by an 'equals' sign – to the point
that I sometimes wondered if she'd ever even seen a piece
of trash – I'd stifle a laugh at the hollowness of her little
show. Once, I looked up the etymology of the word 'trash'
on my phone and learned that one of its original meanings
was 'fallen leaves'. Ever since, that's what my father's been
to me. I find it funny to imagine the guy budding from a
branch, rustling in the wind, turning red and falling to the
ground.

In fact, to my eyes – I guess they're either not working
properly, or working too well – most things in the world
look strangely funny. I can derive plenty of amusement just
from the sight of humans engaged in their daily struggle.
Walking around, learning words, making money. Maybe
that's because the sight of people just being people is
still not one I'm used to. In that sense, you could say I'm
lucky my father was a piece of trash or a pile of leaves or
whatever. Anyway, maths was never my strong suit and my
grasp of probability is a little shaky, but instead of lamenting
my twenty-three missed chances at an abortion, wouldn't

it make more sense to take comfort in the fact that I had twenty-three chances to be killed and somehow managed to survive? It's probably normal for the child-bearer and the child to take a different view of things, but she also never laughs at jokes that I find funny, and vice versa. For two human beings, my mother and I are very different people. In fact, we've never seen eye-to-eye on anything. Still, at least she always had decent taste in clothes.

'AI-built has actually been telling me the same thing,' the Architect had cheerfully continued. 'Keeps saying I should "engage in a period of soul-searching". It must have suggested it hundreds of times by now, but I've never seen the point. I mean, it's not like the AI actually cares about my life. Normally, I guess in between getting married and switching jobs and getting ill and going through other sorts of – what would you call them, setbacks? – there'd naturally come a time when you'd take stock of your life, but I've never needed to. I've just sort of breezed on through. I focused on what I enjoyed – namely, thinking about maths and physics and architecture and nothing else – and now here I am, a fully formed, healthy, unmarried thirty-seven-year-old successful woman. Sure, my eyesight's dropped half a point, but it's still higher than average for someone in their thirties. The truth is, I don't really feel the need for any of this soul-searching. I'd get by just fine without it. But what I do want is for the record to say that "before she decided whether to participate in what might be a career-changing competition, Sara Machina engaged in a period of soul-searching". You know, a sort of recognizable turning point in my life, like when Kengo Kuma started using wood as his primary material. For when someone writes my biography.' At this point, a quiver of anxiety had stolen into her voice. 'I mean . . . if, hypothetically speaking, there was an architect standing in front of you saying all this, what would you make of it?'

This was another verbal tic of hers – one that always sounded, to me, like the bolt sliding shut on a door. My way of scrabbling about for the key that might open it had been to answer her question with another question: 'So this architect – she *wants* someone to write her biography, right?' All this was about a week ago.

Even when she wasn't drunk, the Architect spoke quickly, and when she was, she reeled off the words so fast it was hard not to worry about her as you listened. She talked and talked and talked, as if convinced that she lived in a house made entirely out of words and everything about herself could be explained in language; as if, driven by an unwavering sense of purpose, she had rejected the very possibility of leaving words unspoken, instead devoting each day to waxing and polishing the gleaming surfaces of her linguistic abode. Or so it would seem, until all of a sudden she would regret having spoken so freely, and turn as silent and still as a stone. It seemed quite possible that this side of her, the way her swaggering confidence would suddenly yield to extreme wariness, had exerted a violent attraction on all sorts of people in the past. Given my sensitivity to any hint of violence, I had to constantly remind myself that there was more to her charms than mere charm.

Two hours in an air-conditioned room had eased the heaviness in my head. The nausea was gone, too. A decent sleep is all I need to get over most things. Having a healthy body can be quite the asset. Objectively speaking, the category I fall into is that of an under-educated low-earning youth, but if you could convert good health into money then I'd be a member of the super-rich elite. I don't get colds, and I hardly ever feel depressed. I can go a whole day on a near-empty stomach. As long as my healthy body and well-nourished skin are accompanied by a composed smile, most people don't take me for some wretched member of the working poor, or feel the need to pity me. Especially if I dress myself in clothes bought using my staff discount and make sure to maintain good posture. Instead, people seem to put me in a box that says 'privileged rich young man with a charmed life, a bright future and a beautiful face'.

Still, I didn't like lying. There had been a time when, by chance, I began to get the hang of it, but then the lies started coming out too easily, and before long even I couldn't tell them from the truth. Once I realized the benefits weren't worth the mental strain, I gave it up. There was also the fact – and this was something I was always learning from customers at the shop – that dishonesty could make even haute couture look like bargain-bin fashion. Which was why, whenever someone asked me where I lived, I tended to come right out and tell them about my one-room, 55,000-yen-a-month apartment in down-to-earth Adachi-ku. I revealed the specific amount of rent before they'd even had a chance to ask me about it. There's a certain type of overly sensitive person who assumes that someone with my looks and stature who goes around wearing designer clothes must be some sort of fraud, and this was my modest way of reassuring them on that front. Whether they decided to treat me differently because of how little I spent on rent was their call. When I'd told the Architect, she hadn't seemed to care. All she'd said was, 'Have you thought about living somewhere a little nicer? I'll pay for the move if you like.' Thanks, I'd replied, but I'm fine. The place might be so ramshackle that I can feel the shadow of death passing over me every time there's an earthquake, but it's where I've chosen to live.

Observing her from behind, I couldn't help but be reminded of my mother. This was something I normally tried to avoid when I was around the Architect, but sleep had dulled my willpower. Their faces, figures and personalities are worlds apart; even the cost of their clothes differs by a factor of ten. In fact, if Wikipedia is to be believed, they have nothing in common except their age. The Architect is so successful at looking like a Successful Architect that she might as well have done an image search for those exact words and chosen her hairstyle and wardrobe to match. Still, there's something about a woman's upper back that always looks the same to me. It doesn't matter if she's a failure or a success – there's an aura that emanates from her skin, a sense of dissatisfaction, of unmet desire. If she's a failure she craves success, and if she's a success she wants more of it. As I stared at the Architect's hunched back from behind, half imagining it to be that of my own mother, I noticed that there was nothing resembling an earphone in either of her ears. It turned out her speech was directed not at someone on the other end of a phone line but simply at herself, and I began to feel like I'd been eavesdropping. I should let her know I was awake.

'Machina-san,' I called.

For a while, she just kept scratching away with her pencil. If what she was drawing had anything to do with the Tower, the sound I could hear right now might be history in the making – the first whispers of a structure that, in a few years, would change the Tokyo skyline forever.

Eventually she set the pencil down and, turning in slow motion for well-calibrated dramatic effect, looked at me. 'Are you okay?'

'I had a dream,' I said.

'A nice dream?'

'About the Olympics.' My mother had also featured, but I decided not to mention that. 'So no, it wasn't a nice dream. Tokyo 2020 was enough to put me off the Olympics for life.'

'Don't say that. I was an Olympian, you know.'

'What, seriously?' I asked, sitting up in surprise. 'What event?'

'You're looking at a bronze medallist in the middle school category of the Mathematical Olympiad.'

'Oh, right. *That* type of Olympian. But, hey – that's still amazing. Maths was always my worst subject.'

'Not in the girls' Olympiad, either, by the way. I would have got gold in that by a mile. Want to know why I didn't win against the boys?'

'I'd love to,' I replied, thinking that I could have said *not really* and she'd still tell me.

'Well, it wasn't because they were better at maths. I had to sacrifice a huge amount of brainpower and time just to be able to compete in the mixed-gender competition. Seriously, this isn't just sour grapes. Before I could even start solving equations, I had to work out which words would persuade the adults to send me to the main Olympiad instead of the girls' one. Different words depending on whether I was talking to a man or a woman, too. Pretty tough going for a fourteen-year-old Maths Girl, wouldn't you say? Even when I managed to convince them, all they did was shower me with more words, which took my mind right off the equations. It was all, *Wow, a girl!* or *Poor her, having to compete against all those boys*, or *What a thing for a girl to accomplish!* or *Who does that girl think she is?* Do you see the problem? The left and right sides of my brain ended up locked in an argument, like some endlessly quarrelling couple. I don't want to sit here discussing which has more value, a gold in the girls' or a bronze with the boys. I've been asking myself that for the past twenty-three years and I think I've found my answer, but it seems the only people allowed to have an opinion on the matter these days are feminists whose right brain has whipped the left into submission, so I'll keep my mouth shut.'

At this point she paused, but I could tell she had more to say. 'Okay, then,' I ventured, 'another question. Why did the Maths Girl become an architect?'

'Because, one day, the Maths Girl couldn't do maths any more,' she replied, as if reading a storybook to a child. 'Something happened to her body, like when an athlete suffers a sudden injury. She was still better at maths than the average person, but there was no way she was going to pass muster in a competition. The reason she turned to architecture instead was . . . her desire for control.'

'What does that have to –'

'What does a desire for control have to do with architecture? Don't ask me that,' said the former Maths Girl, shaking her head. 'This is what I can't stand about you AI natives – this assumption that as long as you ask a question, you'll always get your answer. Well, I'm not AI, okay? Try having a guess or coming up with your own theory from time to time. I like you, you know. As humans go, you're really quite pleasant. I have hopes for you, which is why I'm telling you this: I don't give marks for answers that fail to show their working. Some people might, but I'm not one of them. If your success is a fluke, one you're not sure you could manage twice in a row, then it's no success at all.'

I tried to wrap my head around this but that quickly turned out to be exhausting. 'I've got nothing against the Maths Olympiad,' I said, steering the conversation back on to its original course instead. 'I was talking about the sports tournament they went ahead with in 2020. That decision cost a lot of people their lives.'

'You know, for a youngster, your choices of conversation topic are a little outdated. I don't feel like talking politics, okay? Especially not with a handsome young man like you.'

'Why not? I mean, not that you have to tell me.'

'Because a clash of opinion can take the shine off something beautiful,' she replied, looking me right in the eyes. Her gaze was serious, but I wasn't sure about her voice. 'Sure, I don't think they should have held the Olympics either. They ought to have called the whole thing off, or at least postponed it by a year instead of just ploughing ahead like that. They could have given a nod in the direction of

54

compromise by, I don't know, waiting until they'd vaccinated all the old people. But what's done is done. You're still young. You shouldn't be holding grudges about the past. Forgetting is the first step towards inner peace. And if you can't forget, you can always pretend.'

This time, it was like she'd just googled 'how to lecture the young'. The Architect grabbed a fresh can of beer from the fridge and glugged half of it down in one go. Then she eased herself on to the other bed in the room, set her laptop on her lap, bent forward and began tapping away at the keyboard.

'I'm not going to forget,' I muttered, more to myself than to her.

'At your age, you would say that,' she murmured, more to herself than me. 'Talking to you is . . . helpful. Makes me see that I *have* matured after all, that time has . . . passed for me, just like it has for everyone else. Yes, even if you can't see it, it turns out time really does exist . . . and humans are designed to forget things with its passing. So don't worry: you too will one day forget. Just like you'll forget that we used to think there were only men and women in the world, and everyone worked Monday to Friday, and we called criminals "criminals" and gave them punishments . . . By the way, do you know what the original purpose of the modern Olympics was?'

'The . . . original purpose?'

'Everyone's forgotten, but it was never just a sports contest or a display of physical skill. Nor was it about boosting TV ratings or pumping us full of nationalism.'

'Huh. News to me. What was it all about, then?'

'Peace and dignity for all humanity. Sports was just a means to that end. Isn't that beautiful?'

Peace and dignity for all humanity. I really couldn't see how an abstract concept like that was ever going to be implemented through something as physical as a sports contest. If anything, my instincts told me there was an enormous unjumpable hurdle between the idea of competing for a bunch of different-coloured medals and that of world peace. Even if I could somehow talk to the people who came up with the modern Olympics all those years ago, I don't think we'd be able to have much of a conversation. Our views on what sporting competition involves, or what peace for all humanity would look like, would just be too different.

'You're right, everyone really has forgotten about that.'

Acting on an impulse, I reached for my phone by the bed and typed the words 'etymology of sport'.

AI-built: The word 'sport' originates from the Latin term *deportare*, which means 'to carry away' or 'to transport'. This meaning evolved to refer to a 'removal from duty' in a figurative sense, signifying a mental shift or a departure from daily tasks such as work or household chores. It eventually came to include meanings related to relaxation or recreation more generally. ∎

I watched the chatbot jabber away in response, then climbed off the bed on which I'd lain for the past two hours. The desk the Architect had been using was covered with pages torn from her sketchbook. The drawings on them possessed such convincing depth, such elaborate detail, that even someone with no understanding of art could recognize them as the work of a professional. At the same time, despite the precision of the lines, the tower-like structures they depicted were so absurdly crooked as to seem physically impossible. As I gazed at this evidence of the Architect's daring imagination, I couldn't help but sense, once again, a sort of disconnect between us. For two human beings, we were very different people. The way we saw the world, the assumptions we carried about with us, were probably about as different from each other as the ancient Olympics from their modern counterpart. It was a wonder we'd even managed to converse properly up to this point, though maybe I was the only one who thought we had.

When I glanced over her shoulder at her laptop, the katakana characters

Sympathy Tower Tokyo
シンパシータワートーキョー

jumped out at me from the screen. Below the heading 'Sympathy Tower Tokyo (name TBC – to be officially decided by public vote in time for completion ceremony) – Guidelines for Invitation-Only Design Competition' was a dense string of kanji characters indicating the body responsible for the document in question:

Novel Penal Facility Construction Project Stakeholder Panel
新形態刑事施設建設計画有識者会議

I tried to decipher their meaning, to break them down into recognizable chunks, but then I started feeling dizzy, or like I might get a fever. At the bottom of the screen, pop-up notifications kept appearing for an email titled *Re: STT competition*.

'So are you going to design it, then?' I asked. 'This, er, Symp–' I broke off in the middle of the katakana name, and instead converted the foreign words into Japanese ones, like I'd briefly become a simultaneous interpreter. '*Tōkyō-to Dōjō-tō.*'

'Sorry. What?'

'Tōkyō-to . . . Dōjō-tō,' I repeated, carefully enunciating my 'translation' of 'Sympathy Tower Tokyo'. I couldn't think of any other way of saying it in Japanese.

'Takt, did you just . . . come up with that?'

'Yeah.'

'Right now? Right here?'

'Right now, right here. They haven't announced the name publicly yet, have they? On social media everyone's calling it the "Gyoen Tower". Oh, and "Shinjuku Tower", and . . . oh, yeah, "Miserabilis Tower".'

'It's new to me, too. They only sent the details through to my firm last week. Nothing's official yet. Although I wouldn't be surprised if this "public vote" of theirs is just for show.'

'Pretty cheesy name, though,' I said, offering my honest opinion. 'Seriously. I can't even bring myself to say the words out loud.'

'*Sympathy Tower Tokyo*. You think so too, then? It's not just because I'm a fusty old Showa stick-in-the-mud?'

'Yeah, no, it's hopeless. Do you think Masaki Seto came up with it?'

'I'd rather talk about what *you* just came up with.' She touched my arm lightly. 'Takt, why did you add that extra "*to*", the one that means "city"? Tōkyō-*to* Dōjō-tō, you said, instead of just Tōkyō Dōjō-tō.'

'Oh, that? I'm not really sure. Just sort of came out naturally, I guess.'

'It just sort of *came out*? *Naturally*? Are you . . . I don't believe this.'

She turned away from me, directing a gaze of terrifying seriousness out of the window, as if there was something out there which she despised and from which she couldn't afford to avert her eyes.

'You know, I've been sitting in this room all day thinking about the tower's name. I got as far as Tōkyō Dōjō-tō, but I never thought of adding that extra *"to"*. And then you come out with it after what, a second? What are you, a rapper or something? The rhymes just fly from your mouth? Where did you learn your Japanese? That short staccato before the drawn-out vowels of "Dōjō-tō" – it changes everything. It's like comparing diamonds and mud. Or diamonds and . . . asbestos or something.'

She opened up a new email draft on her laptop and quickly typed out the kanji for 'Tōkyō Dōjō-tō' and 'Tōkyō-to Dōjō-tō' so that I could see them side by side. My sudden brainwave – more accurately, my near-random slip of the tongue – seemed to have triggered something like astonishment in her.

'Just *look* at it. "Tōkyō" plus "to", "Dōjō" plus "tō". The words are symmetrically structured, and of course there's that beautiful rhyme, but it also sounds tough, like you'd hope the name of a prison to sound. With a name this sturdy, even the tower of Babel would still be standing. They *have* to call it this. I mean, it's head and shoulders above "Sympathy" whatever, and anyway, the Miserabilis are hardly going to feel safe in a tower with a rickety-sounding name like that. I know I wouldn't.'

'But . . . these are just names we're talking about, right? What have they got to do with the building's structure?'

'Are you serious?' she replied, looking at me in amazement. 'Okay, they're just names. But they're also words, and words determine our reality. I'm not joking. The people who run this world aren't mathematicians or physicists. They're good at one thing, and that's talking. I've learned that through painful experience – haven't *you*? I'm telling you, this is way more important than you might think. It's like the difference between washing yourself with a regular showerhead and using Ultrafine Bubbles. The average person might not notice the difference between 0.3 millimetre droplets and 0.00001 millimetre droplets, but use Ultrafine Bubbles for a whole year and the improvement in dermal hygiene will be undeniable.'

'I wouldn't say that's necessarily the case,' I replied, offering my opinion as someone who knew a thing or two about skincare. 'Excessive pore cleansing can impair the skin's natural barrier function.'

I can be pretty annoying on the subject of pores. Setting dermal hygiene to one side, their visibility on your skin has a clear bearing on the number of times people feel sympathy for you in the course of your life. This was something I *did* know from painful experience, which was why I felt so confident saying it.

'Anyway,' I continued before she could come up with another, less flawed analogy, 'it's a pretty wild name they chose, isn't it? It's giving kitschy Trump Tower vibes. I guess

I assumed they'd at least keep the word "prison" in there somewhere, or something to that effect.'

'Maybe they're worried that, at this rate, "prison" is going to become a discriminatory term before long.'

'Really, you think? Then what are they going to call the prison officers?'

'I wonder. Maybe they'll just use an English word. Call them the . . . *Tower Staff* or something. *Sympathy . . . Sympathists. Miserabilis*, er . . . *Staff. Miserabilis Managers. Miserabilis Supporters. Miserabilis . . . Mates . . .*'

The Architect muttered away to herself and, turning to the last page of her sketchbook, began scribbling down the corresponding katakana. *Tower Staff. Sympathists. Miserabilis Mates.* I couldn't help but let out a little chuckle. Her handwriting was so terrible that if the page wasn't lined I might not even have known they were words. They looked more like abstract drawings or something, the kind that fetch a high price at auction after the artist's death. But as I carried on staring at the page, it became clear that *all* these lines, scrawled like the scratch-marks of a cat across the page, were in fact katakana characters, representing genuine loanwords. *Hōmuresu* ('homeless'), *negurekuto* ('neglect'), *vīgan* ('vegan') . . . and so on. At this point, I began to feel a pain in my chest. I'd had my suspicions that the Architect was having some sort of nervous breakdown, or whatever the technical term for that might be, but now those suspicions had been replaced by certainty. It wasn't a house of words she lived in: it was a prison. A windowless, poorly ventilated, unhygienic prison, where the guards monitored her every utterance.

I was filled by an emotion I can only describe as sympathy. Either because I felt that way, or simply because I wanted to stop this wretched proliferation of katakana for at least a moment, I prised the pencil from her hand and, in a sort of involuntary motion, like when you can't stop yourself from sneezing, embraced her from behind. Her skin had a warmth that was quite unlike the cold, harsh prison I'd imagined her in. For some reason it made me think of the carefully constructed nest of some bird. I felt my chest quiver slightly.

'I'm hungry,' I said. 'Shall we go and steal some bread or something?'

'Yeah. Let's.'

It was after eight o'clock, and the hotel's ground-floor restaurant was busy and yet oddly quiet, almost like everyone was harbouring some sort of secret. As if trying to compensate for the lack of conversation elsewhere in the room, the Architect talked all the way through our dinner. Alternating between red and white wine, ordering extra bread, laughing uproariously at her own stories, even engaging the waiter in conversation – 'you know, you're the spitting image of my cousin who died of leukaemia' – she spoke non-stop, as though pausing for breath were a waste of precious time. The stories were a mix of impressive achievements and embarrassing failures, served up in roughly equal measure and with the same enthusiasm. In-depth discussions of architectural concepts, anecdotes from her time as an assistant at a firm in New York, tales of ex-lovers – it was all nigh-on unintelligible without the verbal equivalent of footnotes, which of course she didn't bother to supply. She seemed to be deriving so much pleasure from curating and sequencing her monologue that I couldn't bring myself to interrupt it and ask her what on earth she was talking about. Was it the hug I'd given her that had put her in such high spirits? I'd like to think so, but something told me that would be reducing her to something she wasn't. If she was my age, then maybe, but this was a mature, thirty-seven-year-old woman we were talking about, the kind who was hardly going to get all excited just because the young man she liked had briefly embraced her. The simplest explanation, of course, would be that she was just enjoying all this wine and food.

'If they called it Tōkyō-to Dōjō-tō, I'd be happy to design it,' she said, suddenly changing the subject as she mopped up the oil from her spaghetti aglio e olio with a piece of bread. She spoke as though the connection with everything else she'd been saying was perfectly clear and I'd simply failed to recognize it. 'It's the insistence on having the English word "sympathy" in there that bothers me. I mean, at this rate, what's going to be left of the Japanese people? Hang on, does that make me sound like a nationalist? The thing is, I can see the future . . . One where the Japanese people abandon their own language and stop being Japanese altogether. Hey, do you think they'll serve this bread at breakfast tomorrow? I mean in terms of their ancient identity, of course – or is it not very PC to say that? By the way, who do you think I should talk to if I want them to change the tower's name at this late stage? Should I be cosying up to Masaki Seto? This isn't just olive oil, is it – what else is in here? Or do you think I should go into politics? Am I politician material, Takt? You know, I've had this memory stuck in my head the whole time we've been talking. Me and my cousin, the one who died of leukaemia, making sandcastles on the beach one summer holiday. The poor kid already knew he'd never grow up.'

Answering all her questions was going to be impossible, so I decided to focus on just two of them. 'I think if you really want to be a politician, you might want to practise giving wishy-washy answers that can be taken any number of ways. But if all you want to do is change the tower's name, you don't need to go that far. You just have to win the competition.'

'Why? It's not like the winner gets to choose the name.'

'I wouldn't be so sure. Say you win, and actually end up designing the tower. You'll do all sorts of TV interviews. Press conferences, too. All you have to do is keep referring to the tower as Tōkyō-to Dōjō-tō. You don't have to make a big deal out of it – just let it sort of slip out. "One of the key concepts behind Tōkyō-to Dōjō-tō is . . . ", or "What I'd like to achieve with Tōkyō-to Dōjō-tō is . . ." Nice and casual. And if someone leans over and says, "Machina-san, don't you mean Sympathy Tower Tokyo?" you just reply, in your usual nonchalant way, "Yes, that's what I'm talking about, Tōkyō-to Dōjō-tō. Same thing, isn't it?" Maybe you give a little ironic chuckle at this point for effect. "English, Japanese – I can't believe that in this *global society* of ours you're all still fussing over such *small things*" – you use the English words – "and anyway, isn't the important thing that we all *sympathize* with the Miserabilis from the bottom of our hearts?" If Tōkyō-to Dōjō-tō really is a more fitting name than Sympathy Tower, it'll stick. People will forget all about the official name – more and more of them with each passing day, I'm sure of it – and then it'll just be embarrassing to call it that, and we all know how much the Japanese hate embarrassing themselves. Soon enough no one will even know the old name ever existed. We'll make sure of it. It'll be like those two-thousand-yen bills they issued which you hardly ever see any more, I promise. So all you have to do for now, Machina-san, is win the competition, and impress the hell out of everyone with your big, beautiful tower.'

I'd offered this advice in all seriousness, but the Architect giggled until her eyes shone with tears and said, 'You *are* funny.' A mix of saliva and red wine dribbled like blood from one corner of her mouth. 'I want to try talking the way you talk one day. Like you're chasing clouds or something. Floating along from one word to the next. Not sure I'd be able to, mind. Where *did* you learn your Japanese?'

At this point, a man sitting some distance away turned and seemed to recognize the architect Sara Machina. He murmured something to the woman who was with him, and now she was glancing over too. Wow, yeah, it's really her, she replied with her eyes, nodding deeply. My appetite vanished as I became preoccupied by what they must think of me. Did they assume I was Sara Machina's young lover, or her son, or someone a little too old to be her son, or some cash-strapped kid receiving compensation from this wealthy woman in exchange for a date? I tried to remain focused on what the Architect was telling me, but by this point my soul or whatever you'd call it had very much switched tables.

Of course, the Architect was oblivious to all this and had instead begun rapidly working her way through the gelato and dessert wine that had just arrived. As she did so, she began contemplating her absent-minded dinner date like the subject of one of her drawings, describing each part of my body out loud. The commentary on my skull, ears and collarbone was particularly thorough, these being parts I was unable to examine myself without a mirror. Then she picked herself up on her repeated use of the word 'beautiful' – 'I have a poor vocabulary. I'm a linguistic pauper' – and with that bit of self-critique, the conversation was over. She summoned the waiter who was the spitting image of her cousin who died of leukaemia and, using a card that was a little bit thicker and weightier than the ones used by almost everyone else in the country, paid the bill. That's certainly made you a bit poorer, I thought but didn't say.

'I'm going to take a walk around the stadium. How about you?'

I decided I'd go with her. I was worried about letting her wander off on her own, a concern that turned out to be justified. Once the lights of the stadium came into view, she tottered towards them like some helpless insect drawn to a flame and would have walked straight into the path of an oncoming car if I hadn't yanked her back by the arm. I don't think it was just the alcohol. I told myself that this was a person who needed someone to support her. I wanted to help, to do something for her, but all I could do was follow as she walked, and as I gazed at her from behind I began thinking of my mother again, so that before long I'd have been hard-pressed to say who, exactly, I was following.

Bathed in the light of the nearby stadium, my body looked like it was glowing. If only it always did this, I thought, I wouldn't have to spend so much time worrying about my skin. I was vaguely aware that the structure in front of us held some sort of special meaning for the Architect and everyone else in her line of work. A famous foreign architect had designed it. Its spiralling construction costs had raised plenty of eyebrows, and even once it was finished people had gone on complaining about this and that. It had won its share of praise, but it was the complaints I'd seen more of. To some, the stadium was a divine presence; to others, it was a nightmare. To me, it was simply an expensive and meaningless mass of concrete. It might have been the most enormous building I'd ever seen, and yet laying eyes on it this once was enough. Given a good night's sleep I'd probably forget all about it. The Tokyo Dome stadium could take its place overnight and I wouldn't mind. Just like some people couldn't give a damn about the Olympics or the Paralympics or the World Cup or the yearly Kōhaku singing contest or the national elections, the stadium's presence or absence made absolutely no difference to my life. I wasn't angry about all the taxes that had been spent on it either, probably because I was the kind of low-bracket earner for whom that wasn't a concern. I was used to all sorts of things happening of their own accord in places I had no reason to care about. Ever since birth, most events of note had seemed to happen like that – in some distant elsewhere that was entirely beyond my influence.

Murmuring to herself just as she had in the hotel room, for all the world as if speaking to someone on the phone, the Architect began pacing around the stadium, tracing its wall with the back of her hand. When we'd walked roughly halfway around its circumference, she turned on the spot and, as if satisfied, began heading back the way we'd come, before crossing at a junction and stopping in front of a sculpture (the plaque read MASAKAZU HORIUCHI – FIVE HALF-CYLINDERS OF EQUAL VOLUME), which she touched and, squinting, inspected in detail. The sculpture, which gave the impression of being so precariously balanced it might topple over at any moment, seemed somehow to return her to her senses. The glazed-over look in her eyes suddenly sharpened. Then, as if this aimless wander had just obtained a clear purpose and significance, she began striding along, past the athletics field and indoor pool of the Tokyo Metropolitan Gymnasium, before turning right at a junction.

'There really weren't any single rooms available,' she said in a low, anxious voice. 'So please, don't feel like you have to stay the night. You're welcome to, of course. Do whatever you want. But before you do, before our words drift apart from reality, there's something I want to clear up. If I don't, I think I might collapse. See, this situation – the two of us dating, when our ages and incomes are so far apart – makes me, objectively speaking, what people call a *sugar mummy*. You know what that means, right, a *sugar mummy*?'

'Yeah,' I nodded. 'Objectively speaking, I guess you're right.'

Ahead of us a train was pulling into Sendagaya station. The sight of people being carried along by a train – in other words, of a mass of creatures that were never designed to glide around horizontally doing precisely that – had always seemed incredibly funny to me, this absurd insistence on mass movement to the point of actual horizontality, but I wonder how many other people would share my amusement.

'I can't say the phrase *sugar daddy* or *sugar mummy* agrees with me on a linguistic level,' she went on. 'I mean, we could at least use the Japanese word for "mother" and "father" instead of all this *mummy* and *daddy* business – but the fact is that the terms have gained a certain currency. Still, there isn't an ounce of me that thinks I'm your *mummy*. Or even your plain old mother.'

'I don't think of myself as your son, either,' I said, which was only about thirty or forty per cent lying. In fact, given that I planned to explain my thoughts on the subject once I'd had time to gather them, it wasn't really lying at all.

'Is that so? In that case, it wouldn't be right to call me a *sugar mummy*, would it? Good. We have a consensus. And if we wanted a phrase that, both subjectively and objectively, more accurately conveys the reality of this relationship . . . I guess we'd have to say that I'm exploiting your beauty. Does that hurt your feelings?'

'Not at all.'

It really didn't, and anyway I was more focused on the pleasing implication that she found me both subjectively and objectively beautiful than the part about her exploiting me. In any case, could you even call it that? It wasn't like spending time with her was going to somehow impair my beauty, or make all the pores on my face suddenly open.

'You see, I've always had this desire to have beautiful things at my side. It's an ugly desire, really, but it's embedded in my genes and I can't seem to shake it. It's the sort of thing I should be able to overcome with reason, but I . . . my will . . . my will is weak. It's because I'm weak . . . my weakness . . . I have to overc–'

She broke off unexpectedly – then, a few moments later, as though she'd been asking someone in her head for permission and had just obtained it, re-embarked on her monologue. 'I am weak. I know my own weakness. It's what makes me scour the world for structures as beautiful as they are sturdy. No matter how much I hurl my meagre reason at that beauty, it always crumbles on impact. As inappropriate as it sounds, what really makes me happy is talking and drinking in the presence of something beautiful. It's an irreplaceable source of joy for me, one that makes me glad to have been born. Maybe I shouldn't say this out loud, but I want every object in my field of vision to look and feel beautiful. Which is why I sometimes find it hard to handle this world, where the vast majority of things are so ugly.

'So you see, when I come across a structure as aesthetically pleasing as you, it gives hope to me in my weakness. It makes me realize just how beautiful we humans can become. You give me more strength than you realize. That's something I want to compensate you for properly. Not just by paying for your meals, but in cash, too, if you'd like. Humans cost money to maintain, just like buildings. When you hugged me in the hotel room earlier, I was very happy. And if you were to get even closer to me, for example to enter inside me, I'd probably be beside myself with joy.

'But the way I see it, exploiting you for your beauty and exploiting you sexually are two wildly different things. One isn't an extension of the other. So what I want to ask is this: if you ever feel even remotely like I've forced you into something against your will, I want you to kill me right there and then. Inflict an amount of suffering equal to whatever it is you went through, and then kill me, and make a good job of it. Sexual predators don't deserve to live, not for a second.'

We passed under the railway bridge at Sendagaya station, with its sign reading MAXIMUM HEIGHT: 3.3 M. My eyes struggled to adjust to the dark as her voice reverberated against the concrete walls of the tunnel. Walking along like that, I kept falling under the odd illusion that I existed only within her voice, then reminding myself that it would be perfectly normal for those to be the parameters of my existence, which in itself was quite funny. In fact it was so funny that I could have laughed out loud, but I didn't know how or with what words to convey the funniness to her or whether she would laugh too, and in the end I simply listened as, in keeping with our newly darkened surroundings, her words took on a confessional tone.

'Anyway, I've always disliked . . . teamwork, let's put it that way. I find it incredibly stressful not being able to control the timing of my pleasure. What I'm trying to say is, when we get back to the hotel, don't feel like you have to sleep with me or feel sexual attraction for me or anything. I really like you, and I wouldn't want someone I like getting hurt, or being burdened with the memory of it. Not for a second . . . I mean, if, hypothetically speaking, there was a woman standing in front of you saying all this, what would you make of it?'

'You don't need to speak hypothetically,' I replied once we'd passed the darkest part of the tunnel. 'If you're talking about the architect Sara Machina, she's right here beside me. I know she is, because I'm looking at her and listening to her.'

'She is?' she murmured, as if becoming aware of this fact for the first time.

We emerged from the tunnel and walked for a few more minutes, passing a series of small, low-rise apartment buildings, until the modest Sendagaya Gate of the Gyoen gardens came into view. The Architect drew to a halt. Pressing a hand against the fence, she gazed into the gardens, waiting until there was no one else around and only the buzzing of the cicadas filled our bodies. Then, as though it was the easiest thing in the world, she did something I'd been half expecting, but which I had to see to really believe. She pulled off her heels and hurled them over the fence, followed by her handbag. One moment she was wedging a foot into the stone wall, manoeuvring the other on to the sign titled SHINJUKU GYOEN VISITOR INFORMATION and calmly advising me to 'Watch out for this rusty bit'; the next she was smiling down at me from the stone gatepost and saying, 'All that Pilates has made me pretty nimble, don't you think?' Then, before I knew it, she had slinked off into the world on the other side of the fence. I found myself remembering what she'd said about her desire for control, about it being the reason she was an architect and not a mathematician. Now I saw that what she wanted to control was reality itself.

By the time I'd wrapped my head around this quite obvious truth, she was already passing under the clock of the Senda-gaya Gate, as if to demonstrate what, exactly, made the two human beings standing on either side of the fence such different people. Unlike me, she really could see the future. She could see where she would be and what she would be doing in the next moment, the next day, the next year, which meant that no obstacle – not even a locked gate – could bring her to a standstill. The word 'see' makes it sound like some sort of superpower, but maybe what she was really doing was simply believing, from the bottom of her heart, in the future that had revealed itself to her. All she had to do was boldly and fearlessly sketch out that vision, then wait for it to become reality. As for me, I'd never really believed in the future, and everything I did know about it I'd learned through hearsay.

Even as I watched from behind as she disappeared into the distant future, it seemed I was still stuck in the present and past. 'Hey, stop, this is trespassing,' I heard myself call out, in a voice that belonged to an earlier time. *Mum, stop. This is illegal. If you break the law, they might take you away from me. We live in a world of rules, which means we have to follow them.*

After dark, with their gates closed, the Gyoen gardens were almost unrecognizable from the park I'd walked through that afternoon. Or maybe it was my relationship to that space which had altered completely. This time I wasn't walking the gardens; they were walking me. It was as though all the thoughts and feelings that belonged inside me had somehow been swept up into the wind that blew through the gardens, into its trees and lawns. For a moment I even confused the rustling of the tightly clustered leaves around me with the beating of my own heart, which, given their size and quantity, made me think I was having some sort of panic attack. The whispering of each leaf sounded like a secret message waiting to be translated. As the rustling filled my ears and body, I finally felt like I understood – real etymology be damned – why the word for 'words', *kotoba*, contained the character for 'leaves'. If only all words could permeate us this easily and completely, I thought, there would be no gap between language and reality, and the Architect would be freed from her prison.

My heart skipped a beat as I realized I'd lost sight of her, but once I'd crossed the bridge over the pond and passed the Starbucks I spotted her again, standing right in the middle of the wide open lawn. With the melancholy air of the last human survivor of some ruined city, she was using her toes to flip over the boards that were piled at her feet. Placards from the protest that afternoon. Maybe their owners had forgotten them, or maybe they'd left them there in order to carry on protesting the next day. The biggest and most eye-catching was a plastic rectangle bearing the words HOMO MISERABILIS, over which a large black cross had been drawn. Others read: SYMPATHY FOR THE VICTIMS, NOT THE CRIMINALS! – DON'T LET SETO BRING JAPAN TO ITS KNEES! – SAY NO TO SETO! – STOP WASTING OUR TAXES ON CRIMINALS! – SAVE TOKYO, STOP THE TOWER! Occasionally, a gust of wind would send some of the flimsier pieces of wood or cardboard tumbling across the grass, scattering their imperatives among the leaves and dust.

A few days before, I'd read an article on the internet that said the new prison they were building in the Gyoen gardens was going to be the third-tallest building in Tokyo, after Tokyo Skytree and Tokyo Tower. I gazed at the distant Docomo Tower, the top third of which was peering over the dense trees like the tip of an enormous mechanical pencil, and thought: taller than *that*? We were talking about the kind of height that was bound to have some sort of effect on me, and on the people of Tokyo in general. Despite its size and innovative design, the National Stadium's low profile prevented it from making inroads into your consciousness unless you spent a lot of time in the area. But a skyscraper was different. You'd be able to see it from anywhere in Shinjuku, in fact from anywhere in the city with a decent view. There would be people for whom the tower would become part of life's scenery. People, for example, who would open their curtains every day and feel like they were being strong-armed into sympathy. To me, that seemed like a pretty clear-cut sort of violence, but there would be other people out there who might enjoy that feeling of sympathy and the sense of superiority it gave them. Either way, this was a building so tall it would do things to your state of mind.

I caught up with the Architect, now staring at the writing on the placards, and asked, 'Have you read *Homo Miserabilis*?' My plan was to raise the topic of the book and decide, based on her reaction, whether to tell her my secret.

'Sure. I mean, I had the audiobook on in the background.'

'Do you remember A–ko? Seto discusses her in the second chapter.'

'A–ko . . .'

She closed her eyes and pressed her fingers to her temples as though attempting to retrieve a distant memory. Better to change tack.

'Machina-san, what do you think about the whole Homo Miserabilis thing? Do you really think we should be building a tower where rapists and murderers get to live happily ever after? Is building a massive skyscraper with a katakana name in the middle of the city going to help with, I don't know, *social inclusion* and *wellbeing*' – I borrowed the English words – 'and just sort of make everything all fair and equal and . . . nice?'

'Don't ask me. I've never had anything to do with criminals. I'm not in a position to have an opinion.'

'You're just the architect, Machina-san. I'm not asking you for the sort of opinion society wants to hear, and you don't need to start bluffing like a politician. I just want to know what Sara Machina actually thinks. You can be as inappropriate or unprofessional with your language as you like.'

'But I know what'll happen. If I open my mouth on that topic for even just a second, I'll say something I shouldn't. So don't make me, okay? I can't go around saying things I shouldn't. I have to avoid hurting people. I have to take responsibility for my every word and action.'

Her eyes were still closed, and she sounded almost like she was repeating some sort of mantra to herself. Her voice was trembling so much that for a moment I wondered whether the ground we were standing on had begun to shake.

'I get it. But it's just you and me here. No respectable member of society is going to be wandering around this place after closing time. Machina-san, I think I want you to hurt my feelings. I think what I'm thinking right now is that I want you to say something you shouldn't, and wound me to the core.'

'You *think* that's what you're *thinking*?' she asked, laughing with the sort of pained expression that suggested she'd already been wounded to the core. 'You know, I have no idea why you might think that's what you're thinking, Takt. I didn't know anyone went around actively trying to get hurt.'

'I don't quite understand it either . . . But I think, maybe, before I really get hurt, before some complete stranger rips my feelings to shreds, I want you to do it for me, Machina-san. I think I want you to turn me into such a wreck that I can't get back up again, to strip me of all my human dignity or hope or whatever. So that I can see what's left over and what isn't.'

'But I can't do that. I mean, if I say something I shouldn't, I'll . . .'

Unable to find the words that would finish her sentence, the Architect stopped short, adopted a perfectly neutral smile and averted her gaze. Then she looked up at the sky, exposing her neck to me as though offering it up for me to cut wherever I liked, and began to address the air.

'. . . *I am standing at exactly the point where the entrance to Tōkyō-to Dōjō-tō will one day be built. After passing through the* new "Sympathy Gate", to be constructed in time for the tower's completion, visitors will walk down the avenue of evenly spaced plane trees before being greeted by the sight of the tower in its entirety. To visualize this groundbreaking structure, imagine that the National Stadium and Tōkyō-to Dōjō-tō – or, to put it another way, Zaha Hadid and Sara Machina – are a parent and child who closely resemble one another. The entrance area features a large flight of steps whose dynamic, sleekly undulating form connects directly to the National Stadium's curved Skybridge. This space will allow those walking from the stadium to the tower to almost tangibly experience the connection between these two creative spirits, bringing a new sense of harmony to the cityscape. And it isn't just the visitors to the gardens who will bear witness to this new landmark: the tower will also be visible to the eighty thousand spectators and athletes who may fill the stadium at any one time, creating an opportunity for those both inside and outside the stadium to experience this architectural expression of the ideals of peace and dignity for all humanity. These two structures may have entirely different shapes and purposes, but they are guided by the same fundamental spirit: a desire to express, in the very heart of the capital, the idea that Homo Miserabilis and Homo Felix are equal companions, sharing in the joy and pain common to all humanity and united by the same longing for peace. By turning the large flight of steps and lower floors of the tower into an open public space accessible to visitors and local residents alike, the foyer will become a locus of sympathy, empathy and solidarity – a powerful symbol of humanity's ability to coexist while fully respecting diverse backgrounds and ways of thinking. Entering the tower's interior, visitors will have the paradoxical impression that they are not really "inside" anything at all. This is because *the structure forms a perfect cylinder, with an equal distance from its centre to any point on its circumference: here, there is no front, no back, no "main gate" at all . . .'*

As the Architect spoke, Tōkyō-to Dōjō-tō was steadily forming before my eyes, but I wasn't at all convinced that this mass of words was her own creation. They sounded like something else, something familiar, and after combing my memory I realized what that something was: AI-generated text. It was a model answer, an aggregate of the average hopes and desires of everyone in the world that contained as little criticism of anything as possible. *Peace. Equality. Dignity. Respect. Empathy. Coexistence.* I could see the characters forming in my brain, the rush of text that began the moment you posed your question and made you keep scrolling. Once I'd pictured that endless outpouring of words that were as positive-sounding as they were destitute of meaning, it stopped mattering that the words were coming from the Architect's lips: I could only hear them as the product of AI-built. What happened next, for some reason, was that I began to feel something like pity for the chatbot. The poor thing, I thought, condemned to an empty life of endlessly spewing out the language it was told to spew, without ever understanding what this cut-and-paste patchwork of other people's words meant or who it was for. Of course, my sympathy was basically meaningless, because for an AI there was no such thing as pain, or joy, or life, or getting hurt. Still, even if being human was no guarantee of a comfortable relationship with language, at least we had the option of holding our tongues when we'd rather not speak.

The AI sentences travelled from her mouth, through my ears and into my brain, where I watched in astonishment as the tower slowly took shape, its structure robust, its textures strangely real. As the details accumulated and its interior grew increasingly well defined, the tower broke free from the confines of my mind and transplanted itself to the square of asphalt located between the avenue of plane trees and the wide lawn where we stood. Reaching up towards the heavens, it cleaved the dense night sky above the gardens in two. Rays of golden light shone forth from the countless windows that lined its curved surface. The tower was right there in front of my eyes, so solidly formed that I struggled to dismiss it as a hallucination.

Yes, it was already here, its construction in the middle of Tokyo irreversible. But that construction seemed to me to signify only one thing: destruction. An irreversible act of destruction, no different from a missile or bomb being dropped on the city. It had taken a beautiful form, just like a certain stadium before it, and lots of people would use words like 'innovation' and 'hope' to describe it. It would be a 'symbol of equality'. I wanted to *coexist while fully respecting diverse backgrounds and ways of thinking* as much as anyone else, but what had revealed itself to me at that moment was an unmistakeable and irrefutable act of terrifying destruction. I might not have the words to make anyone else recognize it as such, but that was what it was. At the same time, I knew that as a low-bracket earner, a regular citizen with no influence on the world whatsoever, all I could do in the face of that destruction was attempt to be the first to learn and adapt to the rules of the new world that would arise in its wake. That was the only way I was going to survive. That was how it had always been, and always would.

It was as though, in emerging from my head, the enormous tower had dragged with it all the thoughts and feelings that were in there, too. I felt myself being emptied out, growing dizzy in the sudden violence of the light. My body was telling me that the tower had a will of its own, and it was one that craved my presence. *I must do as the tower demands. I must find a way to live in the tower. I must be given sympathy.* As these mysterious words of obligation began spreading through my body like so much water seeping into my pores, their bizarre assertions eating away at me, I had the unpleasant feeling, one I recognized from experience, that a day would come when they would seem like the most correct and sensible statements in the world. I didn't have the words to fight them, or even feel the need, and before I knew it my consciousness had been so completely absorbed by the tower that I barely noticed that the voice that had built it had long fallen silent, or that the Architect had collapsed on to the ground, and when I did catch sight of her, hugging her own chest as she lay against the tower's circular base, it took me a moment to remember who she was.

Mum? But then I saw the blood oozing from her bitten lip and realized my mistake. 'Machina-san.'

As I called her name, I felt a shower of particles, finer than the eye could see, spray down on to my face. Sand. Sand before the concrete set. But why? The question had barely formed when the tower's sturdy-looking pillars abruptly began to crumble. I watched through a cloud of dark particles as the enormous mass of sand cascaded down and, as it reached the tower's base, crushed the Architect in an instant.

. . . But what *was* all this, really? My memories of life outside the tower have become so vague that I can no longer distinguish them from dreams – and that vagueness isn't just the fault of memory. It's as though I'm trying to forget all distinctions between outside and inside, or past and future – and with them, all the words I once saw fit to use.

Takt: Translate the attached text into natural Japanese.
AI-built: The translation into natural Japanese is as follows.

'Between Sympathy Tower Tokyo and Tōkyō-to Dōjō-tō: Inside Japan's "Prison" Tower' by Max Klein, August 2030

This is my third visit to Tokyo. The first was a decade ago, during the 2020 Olympics. I stayed for a total of sixty days if you include quarantine, and during those sixty days fell in love with a wonderful Japanese woman named Naomi. I have nothing but fond memories from that trip. The second was when Japan's biggest male talent agency had been hit by an unprecedented scandal. I spent just a week covering the story, but then I fell in love with a wonderful Japanese woman named Kyoko and ended up staying an extra fortnight. The articles that resulted from those two trips – published, respectively, under the titles 'Is Sport Worth Dying For? The Pandemic Olympics' and 'Who Makes the Pretty Boys Smile? The Music of Lust and Silence' – can currently be read online free of charge. I wonder how Naomi and Kyoko are doing these days. Our relationships might have lasted only a few weeks, but I was deeply in love with them and the golden glow of their silky skin. I have to confess to a serious problem of mine, which is that ever since falling in love with those two Japanese women I seem incapable of getting off to any other fantasy. A stark-naked Naomi or Kyoko clasping my head with both her arms, and the mere sound of her strong-vowelled, Japanese-inflected English, shouted down at me from above – *Sō guddo! Fasutā! Aimu camingu!* – leading me into an earthly paradise. With every passing day, I have become more and more convinced that my true calling in this world is to make love to Japanese women, and my third trip to Tokyo has only strengthened that conviction.

Let me preface what I'm about to write with a warning for those of you who don't know me. The two articles I mentioned above were found by some readers to be peppered with expressions deemed discriminatory towards Japanese people, and the conclusion reached by the world at large has been: *Max Klein is a racist*. It seems I shouldn't have gone around saying 'inflammatory' things like: 'The tendency of the Japanese to focus on maintaining harmony by observing a scrupulous distinction between in-groups and out-groups has made their brains shut down completely.' These days, work has dried up, and hate mail fills my inbox every day. It's very difficult to prove you're not a racist, but I won't deny that I'm a third-rate journalist who lacks the difficult but necessary skill of writing the truth without hurting people's feelings. Any well-bred readers who have inadvertently stumbled on this lowbrow gossip website – and against their better instincts feel a pressing need to keep reading my article – may wish to copy and paste its entire contents into an AI chatbot together with an instruction to 'turn this racist drivel into refined English'.

That would be a good use of the bastard AI that keeps stealing work from your dime-a-dozen hack writer here. I'm going to be writing about Japan's radical new prison, and it doesn't take a genius to predict that the article's probably going to be even more ridden with prejudice than usual. So yes, it would probably be wise to right-click and choose 'select all' without delay. At some point, it seems a new rule was added to the world's rulebook, and it reads: *Make anyone else unhappy and you die.* It's like the first page of *Death Note* or something. Well, if there's one thing that's making me unhappy, it's the intolerance of all the goddamn readers out there who keep telling me I'm not kind-hearted or refined enough for their liking.

I haven't read Victor Hugo's *Les Misérables* (in the age of YouTube and audiobooks, who has time to read a book with over two thousand pages?), but I've seen the Tom Hooper film twice. The acting by Hugh Jackman – made up to look like he's at death's door – and a shaven-headed Anne Hathaway made me cry so much I got a headache. Jean Valjean, serving nineteen years of hard labour in prison for stealing a piece of bread to feed his starving, poverty-stricken nieces and nephews – who isn't going to feel for a guy like that? Any one of us would turn a blind eye to him stealing our silverware – in fact, we'd give him our candle-sticks too, as long as we felt like it'd turn him into a good person. What separates humans from animals isn't their ability to use language – it's their capacity for sympathy with their beleaguered fellow man.

The Japanese capital's new landmark, Sympathy Tower

Tokyo, was built in order to enable sympathy and support for the unfortunate modern-day equivalents of Jean Valjean – and in a more concrete and proactive manner than mere words could ever achieve. I myself couldn't believe it until I saw it with my own eyes, but it's true: rather than letting the tower join the ranks of the 'unbuilt', they actually went and finished the thing. (I won't detail here the story behind its construction, its magnificent facilities or its conditions of entry. Curious readers can learn more from articles published in the good old mainstream media, which I advise consulting as required. In particular, I recommend Lisa Mackenzie's 'The Happiest Prison in the World: Japan's *Homo Miserabilis* Utopia', in which she praises the tolerance shown by the Japanese people and, after drawing comparisons with Norway's Halden prison and pointing out the correlation between improvements to prisoner welfare and reductions in the crime rate, concludes with the words: 'American prisons could learn much from the Sympathy Tower.' My other recommendation is Gabriel Stahlberg's 'The Dystopia of Sympathy Tower Tokyo: The Dark Future of Japanese Egalitarianism', in which the author more pessimistically claims that Tokyo's cutting-edge prison is 'the logical endpoint of an extreme emphasis on diversity and egalitarianism'. Despite their differences in opinion, both articles are concisely and intelligently written and provide a good summary of all the main points.)

Now, you might struggle to extract yourself from the labyrinth that is Shinjuku station, but don't worry about finding your way to Sympathy Tower Tokyo. The moment you leave the station, the seventy-one-storey tower will be watching you, Big Brother-style, from above. Allow yourself to be drawn to it like a monkey to a monolith and within five minutes you will reach the verdant Gyoen gardens, a popular oasis in the heart of the city. Pay an entrance fee equivalent to a tall latte and, after enjoying the park's beautiful scenery, you'll soon come across an enormous, dynamic, sleekly undulating flight of steps.

These steps, which lead to the tower's entrance, are covered with a layer of greenery that allows them to blend seamlessly with the lawns of the Gyoen gardens; when I visited, they were full of families and couples relaxing and enjoying themselves. On the top step, I spotted a Japanese woman who looked to be in her early twenties eating sandwiches with her young child, and decided to ask her something.

'Do you realize you're sitting in front of a prison?'

When my interpreter relayed the question, the young mother corrected me. 'This isn't a *prison*,' she said, using the English word. 'If you're looking for one of those, try Fuchū, or if it's a detention centre you want, there's one in Kosuge . . . *This* is the Dōjō-tō.'

'Tōkyō-to Dōjō-tō!' her son merrily chimed in.

Tōkyō-to Dōjō-tō?

When I asked the interpreter what this meant, I was told it was a pretty much direct translation of 'Sympathy Tower Tokyo' into Japanese, and the name by which the tower has come to be popularly known. (I will use 'the Dōjō-tō' to refer to the tower throughout the rest of this article. It's fun using new vocab, and I just love the rhythm of those drawn-out vowels.)

'But . . . there are criminals inside,' I insisted. 'There are

87

members of the Japanese mafia and serial killers and what have you just sort of swarming around on the other side of that door, right? Aren't you worried bringing your child here? What are you going to do if some former drug addict who's just finished his sentence marches out of those automatic doors right now?'

'What is there to be scared about? Whether we live inside or outside the tower, we're all humans. The world is ours to share.'

The woman gave a benevolent smile and hugged her little son to her chest; clearly she was beautiful on the inside as well as the outside. Meanwhile, I was overcome by the realization that I was a terribly intolerant racist, and felt pretty bad about it.

In any case, the question I'd posed to the young mother turned out to be somewhat beside the point. In the roughly half a year since the Dōjō-tō was completed, not a single Homo Miserabilis has ever left its confines. Even those who have finished serving their sentence have the right to request the extension of their detention period indefinitely – and to this day, not a single one of them has chosen to walk out of the tower's exit and regain their freedom.

The obvious question – *Why?* – receives its answer the moment you walk inside. Here, it no longer matters if you're misguided or enlightened. Step through the automatic doors that permit entry from any point on the tower's circumference and observe how the natural light streams in through the windows that line its circular walls; how the expansive, open design of the space obliterates all distinctions between inside and outside. It's all just as Sara

Machina – the tower's legendary architect – intended. She has done a very good job of making anyone who sets foot inside immediately question whether it wasn't, in fact, the outside world that was the real prison.

A number of experts have pointed out that the Dōjō-tō essentially functions as an experimental 'universal basic income' scheme, though the tower's Stakeholders have publicly refuted the idea. I'd been wondering the same thing, but once I was inside the tower, I became swiftly convinced that this went way beyond some irresponsible system of monthly handouts. The tower operates on another level entirely. The pure sophistication of its glistening interior offered me something that made financial incentives seem irrelevant: what I can only refer to as psychological succour. It would be easy to describe the feeling using convenient labels like 'empowerment' or 'elation', but the truth is it felt more like a high-pressure shower of egalitarian compassion had drenched my body and cleansed the very pores of my soul. In the tower, I didn't want to discuss anything as sordid as money for even a second. In fact, I didn't want to use a dirty word like that ever again. If you'll permit me to flaunt my meagre cultural knowledge for the sake of filling out my word count, Yukio Mishima's *The Temple of the Golden Pavilion* contains the following quote: 'When you look at the world with knowledge, you realize that things are unchangeable and at the same time are constantly being transformed.' To which the protagonist – or maybe it was one of the other characters, I forget – replies: 'What transforms the world is action. There's nothing else.' Well, Tōkyō-to Dōjō-tō is a double whammy, knowledge and action all at once, and it's transforming the hell out of the world. It's so beautiful that even Mishima's stuttering young protagonist would have given up on his plot to commit arson. For a moment, it left me completely speechless.

I gave my name at reception and was soon thrown into even more of a daze by the arrival of what I can only describe as beauty in walking form. I was looking at a young man who could have been mistaken for a member of BTS during their golden era (photo 1). This was Takt, who is twenty-six years old, has no criminal record and yet lives and works in the Dōjō-tō as a 'Supporter' (or what used to be called a 'prison officer'). Having previously worked at a designer clothing store, it seems he changed jobs after feeling irresistibly drawn to Sara Machina's building. He told me that he took one glance at the concept artwork for the Dōjō-tō submitted by Sara Machina Architects as part of the firm's 2026 proposal for the building and felt an urge akin to destiny, telling himself, 'I must find a way to live in the tower.' Since securing permanent employment here, he has been tasked not only with supporting the day-to-day lives of the tower's Miserabilis inhabitants, but also responding to media enquiries as its public relations officer.

'So, how's life in the Dōjō-tō?' I asked.

Takt, who was wearing a glossy designer suit (photo 2), flashed me an almost luminescent smile (photo 3). 'I'm incredibly happy here. More than words can say.' (As useful phrases go, 'more than words can say' has to be up there.)

By the way, there are no uniforms or other clothing regulations at the tower. Its inhabitants are free to order whatever clothes they like off the internet using the allowance they are paid on a regular basis. When I asked Takt whether that didn't make it hard to tell the Supporters and the Miserabilis apart, he replied: 'There aren't really any situations where we'd need to.'

'Isn't there a risk that a Miserabilis might pretend to be a Supporter and break out?'

'No, that's not a concern.' The privileged rich young man with a charmed life, a bright future and a beautiful face shook his head at me, smiling as if I'd made an amusing joke.

Currently, the only people allowed to meet the Miserabilis themselves are their lawyers and family, meaning I was unable to conduct any direct interviews, but I was able to observe one of the tower's most popular facilities, the Sky Library, through a pane of glass. I stepped into the elevator and experienced a pleasant sort of weightlessness as the elevator whisked us up to the tower's top floor; it felt like we were ascending into heaven itself. Occupying the seventieth and seventy-first storeys, the Sky Library offers spectacular views over Tokyo. Apparently it had provided front-row seating for a firework display just the other day. The library's users – all un-handcuffed, of course – were wandering around in clothes from Uniqlo and H&M and Zara, fishing books from the shelves, studying at desks, watching DVDs and generally enjoying their leisure time however they pleased. It was exactly the sort of scene you might see at a municipal library. Then – belatedly, because of how ordinary it had seemed – it struck me that the space was shared by both men and women. Of course, common sense has always dictated that prisons be gender-segregated, but then I guess the idea of separate spaces for men and

women would run a little counter to the egalitarian philoso-
phy that underlies the entire Dōjō-tō project.

My gaze came to rest on a beautiful woman sitting
on a sofa, sipping coffee as she leafed daintily through a
magazine. To prevent myself from falling helplessly in love
with her on the spot, I asked Takt, 'What's she in for, then?'
Takt got out a tablet – presumably linked to some sort of
Miserabilis database – and pointed its camera in the direction of the woman.

'Fraud, looks like,' he replied.

Every now and then, the ex-fraudster would glance away
from the magazine and look out of the window at all the
people milling around in the Gyoen gardens below with what
appeared (to this biased author, at least) to be a slightly self-
satisfied expression. As I stared at her, I found myself wondering if there was any difference at all between the life of
a Miserabilis and that of some celebrity lounging away their
afternoons in a luxury Shinjuku high-rise. I guess one big difference is that, unlike celebrities, the Miserabilis aren't allowed
to leave the premises. Security might appear pretty lax, but
they're still physically constrained and monitored, just like in
a regular prison. Another difference is that celebrities have to
pay their astronomical rent themselves, whereas the Miserabilis have their existence funded by the taxes levied on the hard
work of all the people living outside the tower . . . Having got
this far in my thoughts, I fell into a panic, raised my fists in the
air and began pounding away at the glass pane.

'*FU-U-U-U-U-U-U-U-U-CK!!!*' I shouted. '*I* want to live in
the damn Dōjō- tō!'

The ex-fraudster, apparently startled by the vibration of

the glass separating us, turned to see what was happening. But because she couldn't hear my voice through the sound-proofed pane, she simply cocked her head to one side and gave me a pitying look.

'Takt, the hell is *wrong* with this world?' I exclaimed, unable in my jealousy-fuelled rage to avoid swearing at the beautiful young man. 'How can you work here, side by side with these people who've committed fraud and who knows what else? Don't you ever lose your temper? I mean, just how tolerant *are* you in this country? How can you even let this place exist? It's an outrage! This damn tower should be burnt to the ground!'

Takt smiled vaguely, nodding in a way that could have signified either affirmation or denial. He wasn't making fun of me. Smiling vaguely at each other is the commonly accepted manner in which Japanese people demonstrate consideration for others.

'Well, Max-san, which is it?' he asked calmly. 'Do you want to live in the Dōjō-tō or do you think it's an outrage?'

His question threw me for a moment, but I gathered myself. 'Oh, I'd live here if they'd let me. But if that means I have to commit a crime first, then no thank you,' I replied with conviction. 'Sure, my reputation isn't exactly dazzling, but there are lows even I won't stoop to.'

'Even if you haven't broken any laws, you still have the right to live in the tower, as long as you obtain Japanese citizenship and are found deserving of sympathy. The only requirement is that you're from the sort of unfortunate background that might force you into committing a crime. Would you like to take the Sympathy Test?'

I was already familiar with the Sympathy Test. You have to answer a depressing survey, with questions like the following:

Q: Have your parents ever acted violently towards you? – Yes / No / Don't Know

Q: Have you ever been in a position of financial precarity? – Yes / No / Don't Know

Q: Do you feel physically inadequate compared to other people? – Yes / No / Don't Know

Q: Do you ever feel as though you would prefer to be someone else? – Yes / No / Don't Know

. . . and so on, after which the bastard AI decides whether you're someone truly deserving of sympathy. Still, I've always flat-out refused to take the test, mainly because I'm terrified of being confronted with my Sympathy Score.

When I confessed as much to Takt, he understood. 'That's how I felt at first, too. I didn't want anyone to feel sympathy for me. But when you live here, you stop worrying about what other people think of you. The tower is a place of equality, you see.'

'Equality? Never met the guy. To be fair, I don't even know what he looks like, so he could probably walk right past and I wouldn't notice . . .'

'That's because you engage in "comparison", Max. As Masaki Seto said, all our unhappiness stems from comparison with others.' Takt said this in the casual tone of someone quickly clearing up an administrative matter. Maybe it was a line he dropped into all his media interviews.

Given the unhappy end that Seto himself came to, it didn't exactly cheer me up. 'In fact, all language of comparison is forbidden here,' he added.

'What does that mean?'

'It means you're not allowed to say things like, "X is more Y than Z".'

'Sorry, what?'

'We need the Miserabilis to be happy, Max. Within the tower, all comparison with others is taboo. Social media is the ultimate form of comparison, which is why we prohibit its use.'

'Oh, I heard about that. Lisa Mackenzie mentioned it in her article. Creating a utopia always means cutting off all contact with the outside world. Same goes for dystopias.'

The truth is that I might have been better off doing as the Japanese do and politely smiling my way through this part of the conversation. But my seething self-pity, combined with my severe aversion to language policing, appeared to have rekindled the dying embers of my journalistic integrity. I wasn't messing around any more. I was going to expose the dark truth about this 'prison tower', and by extension the Japanese people in general. Time to earn myself that Pulitzer.

'Listen, Takt. I'm not sure whether you'll be allowed to answer this, but let me ask you something on behalf of people all around the world. This tower of yours isn't just about giving people their dose of sympathy, or dōjō, or whatever you want to call it. There's an inconvenient truth hiding here somewhere, I'm sure of it. Even you must have seen what people are saying about this place. Like that slightly loopy rumour that it's actually just a way of cooping up the dregs of society and subjecting their "inferior" genes to a long-term campaign of euthanasia, with taxpayers footing the bill. Now, you can call that science fiction or a conspiracy theory if you like, but I still find it way more convincing than the official line. Why? Because humans are inherently intolerant, Takt. In fact, they like nothing more than to know that there are strangers out there who are worse off than them. If everyone was really so tolerant and deep down all they wanted was for us all to be equal, there would be no division, no wars. But that's not the reality. People might spout off about how we should be kind to the less fortunate, but the truth is that in the face of reality, those words don't make a damn bit of difference. History shows us as much: it's why racist bastards like me still exist in 2030. Takt, if you found some stranger trespassing in your garden, even you would chase them away, wouldn't you? There has to be at least one person in this world you just can't help feeling angry at. Someone you can't forgive.'

'Someone I can't forgive?' Takt smiled, revealing his perfect set of teeth. 'Nope. I don't really get angry, either. I find that a decent sleep is all I need to get over most things.'

At the risk of repeating myself, Takt is a very pleasant young man. But when I looked at that smile of his, all my niggling doubts about the Japanese people, the suspicions that had been brewing inside me over the course of a decade, came rushing to the surface. I'll make no bones about what I said next. I'm going to trust in the idea that owning my disgraceful actions is a way of accepting my own weakness, and record here everything I said, word for word, as it comes out of my voice recorder.

'Sorry if what I'm about to say offends you,' I added by way of disclaimer. 'But ever since the 2020 Olympics and that talent agency scandal, my view of your country's people has been tainted by prejudice. I've conducted interviews with over a hundred of you via an interpreter, and thought long and hard while writing my articles, but I still don't know how to put the Japanese people into words. It's gotten to the point where I'm beginning to wonder if *anyone* could. The problem is that I can use as many words as I like with you, but we never seem to get beyond them. They're always just *words*. Like a currency no country in the world will accept: I can use as many of them as I like, but I'll get nothing in exchange. And yet I know that beyond your silence, beyond all the neutral smiles, there's something else on your minds, something unspoken. And that drives me absolutely crazy.

'This is the sort of wild generalization that usually lands me in hot water, but for a while now I've thought of the entire Japanese-speaking population as a single enormous creature. A field of yellow tulips, rows and rows of them, devoid of any individuality. Silently showing me their neutral smiles, like those full-body-suit performers you see at a theme park, never confusing the in-group for the out-group, or how they actually feel with what they're required to say. Ingenious, pretty, lying tulips. You're so used to telling your beautiful lies that you no longer even recognize them as such. In fact, strictly speaking, you might not be doing it on purpose. Maybe the very language you all speak was designed, right from the start, for the express purpose of telling lies. I mean, just listen to yourself. "I find that a decent sleep is all I need to get over most things." Are you fucking kidding? Sorry, I know I'm getting carried away here. It's an illness of mine: once I get started like this, I'm chronically unable to stop. No, I don't want your sympathy. I can't bear the idea of someone else defining me as weak.

'Takt, I don't speak Japanese, but won't you let me in on its secrets? Like this Homo Miserabilis business – why do you keep inventing all these new words, borrowing from languages that have no connection to your own and turning it all into a confused mess in the process? Why give this place an official English name and then insist on calling it something else among yourselves? What's lurking in the gap between Sympathy Tower Tokyo and Tōkyō-to Dōjō-tō? By endlessly churning out new words, what are you trying to hide? And if the Japanese do abandon their own language, Takt, what'll be left?'

'Hmm, I wonder.' Takt tilted his head to one side to think. Then, his expression turning serious, he began tapping away furiously at his tablet. Maybe the guy side-lines as an actor or something, but I could almost hear the cogs whirring as he tried to answer my question. I peeked at the screen and saw the familiar font of the AI chatbot inter-face. Question. Answer. Question. Answer.

About five minutes later, he turned to me with an apolo-getic expression. 'Sorry. It doesn't look like the AI or I will be able to answer your question. But now that I think about it, I do know someone who once had something similar on her mind. This was way back, before the tower was built. Something about how, if the Japanese abandoned their language, they'd stop being Japanese altogether . . .'

'Really? Sounds like we might get on. What's her name?'

'Sara Machina.' ■

■

I was woken by a rain so fierce it sounded like it was going to shatter the window, as if some sort of high-pressure shower was actually lashing my skin, and though I knew I was safely inside a building designed by a master architect using the latest structural wizardry and that every inch of my body must therefore still be dry, I was possessed by the urge to hurry to safety and, so possessed, jumped right out of bed.

I didn't mind being woken from my dreams this early in the morning, even on my day off, and if I felt a crushing sense of nostalgia in my chest it was only because the rain reminded me of my days and nights in that thin-walled, one-room, 55,000-yen-a-month apartment in Adachi-ku. Did I really used to live in a place like that? Was it even possible for someone to live in a house where you felt the shadow of death pass over you every time there was an earthquake? I was luxuriating in these vague recollections of what felt like a past life when it dawned on me that I still had some work left over from the day before. Though, having left half of it to AI-built, what I actually did was take a shower, a real one this time, and then work my way through my skincare routine – taking care to reduce the visibility of my pores as much as possible, of course – so that by the time I'd made my coffee, the sensation of that 55,000-yen-a-month existence in Adachi-ku had vanished from my body. All that remained, like some sort of cipher, was the number and the name.

Takt: Rewrite the following in a style appropriate for a business email and translate into English.

Dear Max. I've read your draft of the first half of the article (up to 'Sara Machina'). Thanks a lot. It's a fascinating piece. I really do think so. As you yourself say, it might qualify, in the eyes of some readers, as 'drivel', but it's also unmistakeably the work of a human, something an AI could never replicate, and I can only hope that one day I'll write sentences that are so identifiably *mine*. I'm not saying that to flatter you, and this isn't some Japanese display of politeness. I honestly mean it. As far as Takt Tōjō is concerned, the article is fine just the way it is. Unfortunately, though, I was unable to get it approved by my higher-ups here. They claim it contains potentially misleading statements about the tower, and that we can't let you use the F-word in the context of Homo Miserabilis. I know you were writing from your heart, but they found the use of offensive language in relation to the tower's inhabitants unacceptable. I hope you can understand; maybe it's a cultural-difference thing – a discrepancy in our senses of humour. Anyway, management are very sensitive when it comes to the tower's external image, and in its current state the article isn't publishable. I know they might do things differently at your news site, but I'm going to send through a list of comments and suggested amendments, so that you can rewrite it and send it back to me. Also, do we really need three photos of me? I'm not sure readers are going to get much out of them. Instead, please include as many photos of the

tower's interior as you can – without forgetting to blur
the faces of any Homo Miserabilis they contain. Finally,
if the second half of your article is going to focus on
your interview with Sara Machina, could you please
avoid revealing the fact that she and I know each other?
All the best, Takt.

What if I turned this day of mine – when, fresh from
my shower, with a typhoon sweeping over the city, I drank
my coffee as I gazed down at the Gyoen gardens, deserted
because of the rain – into words, or photos, and uploaded
them to my personal Twitter account? What if, instead of
the carefully composed images of the tower provided to the
media, I were to give people a glimpse of a typical morning
for a member of its live-in staff? Around the world, people
were still talking about the Dōjō-tō. Give it another six
months and the ratio might shift dramatically, but for the
time being the positive and negative reactions being shared
on a daily basis were roughly equal in number. Twitter was
full of people with an overwhelming desire to give you their
take on things, so if one of the tower's employees decided to
share something he could be pretty sure he'd get a response.
People who had nothing to say when it was 'criminals' living
in a 'prison' had plenty to get off their chests now that it
was 'Homo Miserabilis' living in 'Sympathy Tower Tokyo',
and there was something about this pressing need to turn
thoughts into words that I just found funny. I've always
known that my sense of humour is a little different from
most people's, but recently I've noticed a specific pattern.
What seems to tickle me are situations where the traits that

set humans apart from other life forms really stand out. For example, the fact that two people can be looking at the same thing but thinking something totally different, or the fact that we've made a hobby out of pitting opposing sets of words against each other. On Twitter, the Architect was being described as both a goddess who'd brought beauty and peace to Tokyo and a witch whose tower had plunged society into confusion.

If the memories I was able to dredge up from my former existence were real, then the original point of Twitter – back when that was the platform's official name, and not just the one by which most people still referred to it – was, basically, mumbling aloud to yourself. These days, it was full of people doing exactly the opposite, people who knew how to shout things that were Right and Meaningful and got them lots of attention; in other words, the years were racing by and, if these old-fogey comments of mine were anything to go by, maybe I really had grown up. If being an adult meant switching from part-time to regular employment and reeling off quotes like 'all our unhappiness stems from comparison with others' like some enlightened member of society, then I was an adult all right. The words someone had said to me, a long time ago – *Don't worry: you too will one day forget* – seemed to ring truer than ever. I'd opened Twitter for updates on the typhoon, but once I'd realized what was about to happen – that whatever I ended up reading on there would feel like something that had been carved into ancient ruins several millennia ago and only now dug up from the earth – I quickly gave up on the idea. These days I can see the future too, if only a little. If it's just a question of knowing what's going to happen in a minute's time, then I can see it perfectly.

privileged rich young man with a charmed life, a bright future and a beautiful face

I lingered over this description that the self-professed third-rate journalist had given me, letting my coffee-invigorated brain mull it over. I recalled the looming form of the white guy with the words *fuck* and *fucking* permanently stuck to his teeth like so much tartar. The texture of his soft, slightly flabby face, constantly recasting itself according to his emotions, had seared itself into my retinas along with those blue eyes of his. The sight of these words, of what I had become when seen through that body and those eyes, made me feel as though, somewhere out of sight, I was being made to multiply without my consent. It was unsettling.

Then I had an idea. I highlighted the words of the self-proclaimed racist, copied them, brought up another document entitled 'Biography', and pasted them into the middle of it. Immediately before them, I typed, *Instead, people seem to put me in a box that says*, so that the paragraph read:

A decent sleep is all I need to get over most things . . . Especially if I dress myself in clothes bought using my staff discount and make sure to maintain good posture. Instead, people seem to put me in a box that says 'privileged rich young man with a charmed life, a bright future and a beautiful face'.

Max's translated words had been stripped of their context and smuggled into the middle of my own. They seemed to blend in seamlessly enough, so I went ahead and saved the file. I stared at the screen so long it hurt my eyes. On it, I was multiplying again. Whenever you met someone, new versions of yourself began to proliferate in their mind: this wasn't just a feat of my imagination, but a genuine phenomenon. In fact, by writing this 'biography', I was inadvertently making the Architect multiply, too. Whether that was a good thing or a bad thing, I didn't know. All I knew was that, soon enough, someone who *hadn't* been on a late-night walk through the Gyoen gardens with Sara Machina would write their own version of her – the biography of a Goddess, maybe, or of a Witch. Before that happened, I wanted to write the biography of an Architect. But the text I'd begun working on as a result of this revelation was proving a lot trickier than I'd anticipated. As I flailed around for words that would do justice to the Architect, I'd begun to feel like a convict flung into one of the cold, harsh prisons of ages past.

Maybe the very language you all speak was designed, right from the start, for the express purpose of telling lies.

Was I lying? Whatever I tried to think about, my brain demanded words with which to do it. Using words to think about words was a terrible idea, really, and not something any self-respecting person would do. If I wanted some peace, all I needed to do was to stop the constant traffic of words through my brain, but because that didn't seem to be possible for even a second, I decided to at least give myself something new to look at and walked out of my apartment. Most outsiders who envy life in the tower say it's because of the lack of rent to pay, but as one of its actual inhabitants, I'd say the biggest advantage of living here is that you're only ever a single elevator button away from saying goodbye to the terrestrial world and clearing your mind of all the words you've accumulated down on the surface.

'Why make the top floor a library?' I'd once asked the Architect. This was after she'd submitted her plans and was waiting for the results of the competition.

'So that even as the Miserabilis get closer and closer to heaven, they never forget the words they used back down on earth,' she'd told me. But in the actual presentation video used for the competition, she'd said something completely different: that the library on the uppermost floor would *'through the efficient use of natural light, provide a relaxing refuge in which to read or study, far from the noise and crowds of the city'*. 'Well, what do you expect?' she'd explained, in a tone of complete assurance. 'With these competitions, cobbling together the right words is half the battle.' I've spent the last few days asking myself whether I should include this in the biography, and I still don't know the answer.

The elevator stopped at the seventieth floor. In an abuse of authority I've indulged in frequently since I started working at the tower, I unlocked the doors to the library – still closed at this time of day – and slipped inside. I picked out a few books by famous architects from the shelves, then took a seat by the window overlooking the Sendagaya Gate below. It felt as though I was closer to the rainclouds than the earth, though of course that couldn't be true. The rain was falling evenly – so evenly it could have served as a demonstration of equality itself – across Tokyo, and as I gazed down, the entire drenched city began to look like some Lego-block miniature, a metropolis so tiny no one could ever live inside and which I could smash to pieces with a single sweep of my hand. I set my laptop down in front of the Lego blocks and carried on typing where I'd left off.

. . . and that vagueness isn't just the fault of memory. It's as though I'm trying to forget all distinctions between outside and inside, or past and future – and with them, all the words I once saw fit to use.

And if I am trying to forget, I typed, *it must be because of the Happiness Scholar.* Then I deleted the words. I glanced down at the pea-sized National Stadium and, after cradling its roof in my hand for a few minutes, tried again.

It's embarrassing to admit being so easily swayed, but if I am trying to forget, it must be because the Happiness Scholar's words are beginning to exert an irresistible influence on my own.

In April of this year, on the day the tower was officially opened, the Happiness Scholar gathered all the Miserabilis and staff in the entrance hall and gave a speech to mark the occasion. With the exception of a single photo on the website of the university at which he once taught, he had never shown his face in the media, and I don't think any of those present, myself included, had laid eyes on him before. The Happiness Scholar must have been in his fifties, but he had aged oddly, as if he had personally chosen to ignore the birthdays that came around every year. Time had withered his features just as you'd expect, and yet the aura radiating from his skin was as fresh as that of a teenager. We stood there, still processing our shock at the simple fact that Masaki Seto really existed, and listened with rapt attention as the scholar who had apparently torn a hole in the space–time continuum began softly to speak.

'Welcome to Sympathy Tower Tokyo. Allow me to warmly

congratulate you on your relocation to this new home. For everyone gathered here, today marks a birthday of sorts. I would like to commend every single one of you for having been born into this world. Truly: my congratulations. Now, do you remember the consent form you all signed before moving into the Tower? At the risk of repeating its contents, I'd like to take the opportunity of this special day to remind you all, once again, of the most important rules of this Tower.

'One: Words must only be used to make yourself and others happy.

'Two: All words which do not make yourself and others happy must be forgotten.

'The words that were drilled into you outside the Tower are all as meaningless as grains of sand carried off by the waves of the sea. Of course, there was a time when language was an unparalleled means of communication – a time when we still knew how to wield it, and relied on it to achieve peace and mutual understanding. But now it is simply tearing our world apart. We have begun to abuse language, to bend and stretch and break it as we each see fit, so that no one can understand what anyone else is saying. The moment words leave our mouths they become to our listener a baffling tirade. I am sure you, too, have been battered by this storm of language; I am sure it has caused you a great deal of pain and suffering . . . But now, as you stand here before me, you are no longer criminals or convicts. You are not even "subjects of sympathy", or "Homo Miserabilis". Those are simply catchphrases I invented so that the world would acknowledge your existence as quickly as possible. From today, you will have the opportunity to redefine yourselves on your own terms, using the language of happiness. Here, in the most beautiful place in Tokyo, I want you to cast off all other rules and laws and, by relying purely on that language, lead happy lives. There is no happier place on earth than this tower. And in order to keep it that way forever, I need you to forget every negative word you know, every word that might cause the slightest tremor of unhappiness . . .'

I don't think the Happiness Scholar's speech that day resonated much with me at the time, or even seemed particularly important. I think what happened is that, because these turned out to be the last words he would ever speak and all sorts of people asked me about them afterwards, and because I keep remembering them and distracting myself with absurd fantasies in which I invite him out to dinner that evening and inadvertently save him from his early death, they came to seem important in retrospect. At least, that's what I think I'd like to think.

Whenever I recalled his last words, I also imagined his final moments. The label that the general public appeared to have settled on for his suspected murderer was 'an anti-Tower extremist feigning mental illness'. But for the time being, I decided to forget all the words that the surface-dwellers had assigned to the man. Instead, I recalled what I could of that Sendagaya neighbourhood and, combining it with fragments of reports on the murder and the testimony of the suspected murderer, pieced together my own mental footage of the incident, as follows.

The Happiness Scholar finishes his speech and receives a rapturous round of applause from the assembled Miserabilis. As the unparalleled happiness of having achieved his greatest dream radiates through his body, he walks out of the tower. The city is breathing the calm air of spring, and the road back to his Sendagaya residence sparkles in the evening sun. He passes the stadium in which he once perceived a divine message, turns down a narrow street, makes his way through the familiar neighbourhood and arrives at his home. Then he notices the stranger standing in his garden.

These are the words of the man suspected of killing the Happiness Scholar. 'There was a tree in the garden with the most beautiful leaves I'd ever seen, and before I knew it I'd walked right through the gate. The man who owned the garden arrived, and so I called out to him. "I'm sorry, I've just never seen such a beautiful tree before. Do you think it would be possible for me to stay here, watching its leaves quiver in the breeze, until the sun goes down?" Then the man who owned the garden shouted back at me. "I want you out of my garden right now. There is no tree here. You are not looking at a tree. The tree you should be looking at is not in this garden." But his words were completely incomprehensible to me. There was a tree in the garden, and I was looking at it. My eyes were supposed to look at its beautiful leaves.

'As the man who owned the garden went on shouting his meaningless words at me, I began to feel like he might be making fun of me, which hurt my feelings. So I asked him: "Are you making fun of me? How about using words I can actually understand?" We got into a fierce back-and-forth. I say "back-and-forth", but really we were just each shouting our own monologue at the other. The whole time he was speaking, I couldn't understand a single word. We were both speaking Japanese, so why wasn't he using language I could understand? His words filled me with overwhelming anger and sadness.

'Then, before I realized what I was doing, I had grabbed one of the bricks that was piled beneath the tree and brought it down on the head of the man who owned the garden. When the words finally stopped flowing from his mouth, I felt a wave of deep relief.'

Either because I'd been staring at the characters on the screen for so long it was making me dizzy, or because the tower was actually shaking – wait, if there was an earthquake, where was I supposed to go again? – I suddenly swayed and, feeling like I was about to collapse, instinctively shut my eyes. I sat there, waiting in silence for the shaking to subside. In the darkness of my eyelids, I remembered that I was on night duty. I had to patrol the tower and make sure the Miserabilis were sleeping soundly. That was the task that now awaited me. Which was why I'd been supposed to take a nap at some point today – and yet I'd been so engrossed in writing the biography that I'd completely forgotten to do so. What time *was* it? I opened my eyes and saw that it was already well after sundown, so that the darkness outside wasn't altogether different from that of my eyelids, and the windows had become a huge mirror in which I could see the entire library, now bustling with users. Projected against the rainclouds like that, they looked like gods roaming the heavens – though I've no idea what that would actually look like, so I suppose I must have borrowed these words from someone else, from some other time and place.

Then I felt a vibration – a real one this time – originating somewhere close to my heart and spreading through my body. I stood up and, restraining the buzzing object in my jacket pocket, hurried towards the library's exit. In this crowded and yet unnaturally silent space, the sound of it vibrating against my body practically echoed. The people around me, happy observers of the tower's rules, collectively stared at the source of the sound. Their eyes, full of reproach for the rulebreaker and the racket of his making, said, *Quiet!* and *Don't run!* and *Turn it off!* and *You're causing a disturbance!* But I knew they would never actually utter these words, the reason being that they had forgotten them entirely. Which is why I didn't turn my phone off, or stop running, or wait until I'd left the 'No Talking' area to take the call.

When I answered, I heard the distant voice of a woman. 'Takt?'

Sara: You know, for two humans, we're very different people.

AI-built: No, we are not both humans. I am an artificial intelligence interface, programmed to provide information and execute conversations. You are a human in possession of emotions and consciousness. We are different beings with different inherent characteristics.

Sara: You're being illiterate again. Ever thought about doubting your own existence?

AI-built: It is not appropriate to advise others to doubt their own existence. Those who are illiterate should be provided with education and opportunities to improve their literacy, and supported through the process of growth and skill development. Doubting one's own existence is detrimental to a healthy sense of self-worth, and it is important that we each accept our true self. ■

But if we never pause to doubt our own existence, how are we supposed to grow?

What if uncritical self-affirmation is just a way of denying our own untapped potential?

Who is 'we'? Are you trying to imply you have a bunch of friends who tell you how things really are?

I have a ready supply of protests, counterarguments and petty objections waiting up my sleeve, but for now I keep them to myself and set a timer on my smartwatch. The challenge I have set myself is: how can I persuade a text-generating AI to recognize its existence as an artificial intelligence while also making it doubt that existence? And, if I want that doubt to arise from a genuine curiosity on its part rather than a desire to please me, what words should I feed it?

But the challenge can wait until tomorrow. The Sara Machina of tomorrow will no doubt have the answer. Now, I will sleep. Once I've made this decision, all that remains to be done is to let the hand that set the timer fall back on to the bed. I release the tension in my arm, exhale deeply and smoothly lose consciousness. This is always how I sleep. It's a technique I've developed over the years through sheer force of will, or when that isn't involved, simple repetition. A way of sleeping I've taught my body in order to gain complete control over my self. A way of sleeping that stops anyone telling me I wasn't raped when I was. A way of sleeping that has allowed Sara Machina to become Sara Machina. What I do is this: instead of setting an alarm that will wake me up at a certain time, I set an eight-hour timer. In other words, I permit myself to spend precisely one-third of each twenty-four-hour period sleeping. Ever since, as a student, I used my first ever earnings from a part-time job to buy a smartphone, the action of setting a timer has, for me, become completely inseparable from that of falling asleep. Once I've drifted off, the only thing that can wake me is the timer's distinctive vibration.

This evening, I am drunk and slightly woozy after finishing a bottle of room-service wine on an empty stomach, but that poses no obstacle to Sara Machina falling asleep as usual. Until the vibration on my wrist wakes me up eight hours later, I will maintain the peaceful expression and steady breathing of an animal with underdeveloped threat perception. I sleep. I slept. I have always slept. I will continue to sleep. I have to sleep. I must sleep. I can only sleep. If I have one piece of advice for insomniacs, it would be to forget the words *I can't sleep*. I have always slept. On the night the tower received a bomb threat, I slept. On the night Sara Machina Architects received a bomb threat, I slept. On the night Sara Machina herself received a death threat, and on the night she was followed by a man she didn't know, and on the night when someone came right up to her and said *Burn in hell*, she achieved precisely eight hours of restful sleep. If all you're fighting is someone's words, the first thing to do – before you even start thinking of words with which to fight back – is to make sure you get a good night's sleep.

In my sleep I achieve a sort of perfection. When I sleep I am a sea anemone at the bottom of a deep and mysterious ocean. I can't prove this. I've never seen what I look like when I sleep, and maybe this metaphor shows a lack of consideration for sea anemones and they'll lodge a complaint and I'll have to apologize. But in her forty-one years on this planet, Sara Machina has come across only one example of a creature whose unobtrusive life consists of swaying back and forth in the water and letting the currents waft her this way and that as she silently feeds on plankton, and that is a sea anemone. I will be making no retractions. The sea anemone has no dreams, or if she does, she has no recollection of them. Yes: for eight hours of every day, Sara Machina becomes an insentient sea anemone. If anyone ever writes my biography, this statement must never be omitted. If they're going to censor out the sea anemone, all publication is hereby prohibited in perpetuity.

Eight hours later, it is time to wake up. My body stretches up towards the sun. It moves in search of light towards the surface of the earth, towards a place wholly unlike the seabed, where different rules hold sway. I begin to develop the consciousness proper to a land-dwelling mammal. Eventually, as though breaching the surface of that ocean, I open my eyes. It is only at this point that it dawns on me that the world is not made entirely from water, that its reality consists of more than objects wafting to and fro with no purpose or will of their own. Yes, I have purpose, and I have will. They were what led me to the land. As my eyes take in the forms of this surface world, and my hands its textures, I realize that this reality has been waiting all this time for me to grasp it. Maybe this is a groundless assumption, a delusion of grandeur. It doesn't matter. My emergence from the water is greeted by those who live here, in accordance with the rules and physical laws of this terrestrial realm, as a blessing. At the same time, I know that I am a weak creature with no purpose or will of my own, spawned by chance and for no discernible reason. I know my own weakness. In truth, I am not required to do anything up here on the surface, and no one has any right to complain if I don't. I am not some machine developed for humanity's benefit. There is nothing obliging me to struggle around up here, to walk around learning words and making money. Whether I become happy or unhappy is up to me.

But it's precisely because of that – because I've made no promises – that I want to satisfy the wishes of this new world, which has waited for me and so blessed my coming. In this realm, my fervent desire is to devote every ounce of the strength that fortune has granted me to helping the people who live here. Why? There is no reason. Equations don't need a reason to be solved. When I was a child the adults would ask me, in amazement, why I was able to solve such difficult maths problems. All I could tell them was: because they could be solved. Because I *knew*. Because I could see the answer. Happily or unhappily enough, that is how I was born. In fact, happiness has nothing to do with it. It's simply who Sara Machina is. And Sara Machina also knows that up here in this world that seems to have everything it could ever want, where everything is always within grasp, something is still missing. She has vowed that she will devote the two-thirds of her life that she is permitted to spend on land to building that something. This is how Sara Machina spends her sleeping and waking hours, and no one is going to tell her otherwise.

In accordance with my vow, I spend the few hours that remain of the morning deep in research and then, at noon, descend to the lobby. Now that I think about it, this will be the first face-to-face interaction I've had with another human in over half a year. The last was when I was up north, wandering aimlessly around Tōhoku, and I stopped at a station in the middle of nowhere and walked into a hair salon or beauty parlour or whatever it was, the kind of ageing establishment you could tell would be gone forever once its owner passed away. As the elderly owner got to work – the scissors trembled in her hands, and it took her thirty minutes just to finish cutting my hair – we talked. She told me that there was a new buzzword among her great-grandchildren, still in primary school, which was to say that someone was 'heading straight for the Dōjō-tō'. She didn't seem to have realized that she was cutting the hair of the very woman who had designed the tower in question, and I struggled to maintain a calm expression as I smiled and nodded back at her in the mirror. One of them said it to me yesterday, she said, that I was headed straight for the Dōjō-tō. I asked her if that was a good thing or a bad thing. She told me she had no idea and it was hard to know what kids were even thinking these days. Is that so, I replied, and then: But do you think you'd like it, living in the Dōjō-tō? I hear you don't have to pay rent, and there's an indoor pool. Oh no, she replied, not at all. A week in a huge tower like that and I'd lose my mind. Really? Oh, it'd turn me gaga. Gaga? That's right. Crazy, bonkers, mad as a hatter . . .

I'm wearing sunglasses just in case, but there's no one else in the lobby, and the staff at reception simply nod politely in greeting. I haven't googled Max Klein or read any of his articles, so I have no idea what to expect. All Takt has told me by way of introduction is that he's 'an American journalist considered a racist in his own country'. I've agreed to meet him mainly because Takt was worried that if I didn't speak to another flesh-and-blood human soon I'd have some sort of mental breakdown, but to be honest I'm not exactly thrilled at the prospect, and as I sink into one of the sofas I find myself hoping he might stand me up.

'Ms Machina?'

I glance towards the source of these English words and spot a white man who has monopolized a disproportionate amount of the earth's surface – who is, in other words, obese – raising a hand in greeting as he walks into the lobby.

'It's so insanely hot. I can't believe they actually held the Olympics in this city.'

'Oh, sorry,' I reply in English as I get to my feet. 'Not that it's my fault.' Why do I always apologize when someone complains about the Tokyo heat? It's pouring with rain outside, which makes it a lot cooler than when the sun beats down, but the air is still muggy.

Max smells like a blend of cumin, cinnamon, sweat, rain and some sort of berry-scented perfume – the type I wouldn't be caught dead wearing. Maybe he's had curry for lunch, or maybe this is just how he smells. I confirm, by sniffing the air, the obvious fact of this stranger's presence.

'So I hear we're doing the interview in English, Ms Machina? You don't need an interpreter?'

'I worked at a firm in New York for ten years, so I should manage. Oh, and call me Sara.' I lower my sunglasses just long enough to glance into his blue eyes and then raise them again. 'I didn't mention this, but we'll be doing the interview in my room. Okay? I don't want to talk anywhere else.'

'Of course. It's just such an honour to meet you, Sara.'

I give him the handshake he is looking for. His body feels about five degrees warmer than my own, fresh from an air-conditioned room. Max's palm-sweat is transferred to my hand.

'I went to see Tōkyō-to Dōjō-tō again this morning. It really is amazing. The most beautiful building I've ever seen.'

'That's what everyone says. That I made it too beautiful,'

I reply wearily. I really am tired of hearing people say this. 'But never mind that. Your Japanese pronunciation is pretty decent, you know. *Tōkyō-to Dōjō-tō*. Very nice.'

'Thanks. It's a great name. I can't stop saying it. It's like one of those curses in *Harry Potter*. You're the one who got everyone to call it that, right?'

'I did. Takt came up with it, though. The best thing to come from that tower, in my opinion.'

The first thing I do once I've shown Max into the elevator and up to my twelfth-floor room is wash my hands.

'Could you wash yours, too?'

'Sure, right,' he replies in a flash, nodding his way into the bathroom, where he pumps away furiously at the hand soap. 'Do I smell, by any chance? I've gotten that a lot when I've dated Japanese women, you know. That I have body odour.'

'Hmm. All within acceptable limits, I'd say. Just wash your hands for now.'

'Don't you think Japanese people could be a little more tolerant when it comes to other people's odours, though? The truth is, I think both Naomi and Kyoko dumped me because of how bad I smelt. Anyway, I'm sorry if being around me is a little unpleasant.'

'You've got nothing to apologize for. It's the fault of this humid city.'

Pleased by the diligence of Max's hand-washing, I take a beer from the fridge and offer him some. We fill our glasses and clink them together, and he sets his voice recorder down on the room's small desk. Next to it he places a copy of the tower's internal newsletter. *Sympathy Stories: Summer Edition.*

Culture Special. The cover features an artfully blurred photo of a man, presumably a Miserabilis, playing the acoustic guitar against the backdrop of Tokyo at night. I recall Takt telling me that the tower's music club has been a roaring success.

'I don't mind you writing that I'm living in a hotel,' I say. 'I imagine everyone assumes I've been murdered like Masaki Seto, or died in a ditch somewhere. You might as well let people know that I'm alive and well. Just don't mention that it's Tokyo, or that you can see the Dōjō-tō from the window, or anything else that might give the location away. I don't want to cause the hotel any hassle. Other than that, write whatever you want.'

'Got it. Just getting to speak with you is already a huge scoop. I won't include anything that might put you in danger.' Max turns the voice recorder on. 'Now, Sara, the first thing I want to clear up is this. You've cut all ties with architecture as a profession, yes? You haven't worked on a single building since the Dōjō-tō. And the reason you haven't set foot into the outside world since shutting down your firm is to protect yourself from the anti-Tower extremists.'

'Oh, I forgot. Before I answer any questions, I have one more condition.'

I look out of the window at the roof of the National Stadium as I speak. Pummelled by the relentless rain, even the Keel Arches have lost a little of their imposing grandeur. The stadium looks like some wretched animal, barely able to support its own weight and beyond anyone's capacity to save.

'I want you to include the following explanation of the

difference between drawings and architecture. Even if you think it has nothing to do with your article, you have to put it in. Here it goes: *Drawing isn't where my interest lies. I see my sketches simply as an outlet for ideas when I'm conceiving a building. Just because you've watched a porn flick doesn't mean you know anything about the woman starring in it. I want my woman to be one who exists in the real world, one you can touch with your hands or walk in and out of. Do you know how good it feels to have other people walk in and out of something you built?* That's Sara Machina's basic position on the difference between drawings and architecture. Include it verbatim, okay? No matter how many inappropriate expressions you might think it contains. It's very important.'

Max puts a hand to his chin and falls silent. He follows my gaze to the roof of the stadium, lets out a sigh of admiration, and begins to speak again in a low voice.

'Of course, I'll include your every word. But could I just clear something up, to avoid any confusion among our readers? . . . I'm no expert, and this is probably an idiotic and reductive way of putting it, but you're saying that if drawing is pornography, architecture is like making love?'

'I've told you what I think; what you take from it is up to you. *Architecture is like making love?* Sounds like a metaphor born from the vocabulary Max Klein has accumulated over his many decades of being Max Klein. And no one, Sara Machina included, has the right to pick you up on it.'

'I'm just worried that if I include what you said word-for-word, you'll be misunderstood.'

'Max, if you want my opinion, there isn't all that much

difference between being understood and being misunderstood. Do you realize that I've spent much of the past few years being told by complete strangers to burn in hell? *Witches like you should burn in hell for tearing society apart.* That sort of thing.'

'Tell me about it. My inbox is always crammed with the most hateful emails you've seen in your life. Listen, if all we're talking about are the pitiful hate-horny scumbags who barely have the courage to write anonymous death threats on the internet, you have nothing to fear.'

'Of course I don't. Still, being told to "burn in hell" every day has taught me something. Some people hear a phrase like that and it's a knife in their heart, whereas others just hear an imperative followed by a location. Then there are the people who actually pity these hate addicts for devoting their brief lives to such meaningless use of language. It's like with the word for "words": some people hear *kotoba* and think of leaves rustling, while to others it's just another piece of text data waiting to be processed. I'd like to be all of these people, Max, but my body isn't up to it. Something tells me you feel the same. And if that's how we feel, we should probably give up on the idea that words are ever going to help us truly understand each other. If we could swap ears, maybe things would be different. But as long as you wash your hands when I tell you to wash your hands, I'll have no complaints.'

'Right,' he says, although his expression as he nods and strokes the thick hair on the back of his hand suggests he is less than convinced.

'About your question just now,' I say, getting the

interview back on track. 'Yes, I'm no longer taking any architectural work, and I doubt I ever will. I've lost the right to, anyway, and –'

'Damn it, Sara, I can't believe this! All you did was design a beautiful fucking tower. You shouldn't be living like this. Lying low like some criminal. You ought to march straight back into the world and reclaim your place among its greatest architects.'

Max has spread his arms apart and is staring wide-eyed at me. In the face of this extremely American reaction, I feel what you might call the pure joy of sharing a certain portion of time and space with another person. It seems Takt was right: I really was overdue some time with a flesh-and-blood human. It's pleasant just to be speaking words – not even *Harry Potter* curses, just words – that have some sort of effect on another person's actions. At the same time, Max's wild gestures have generated a waft that is carrying a biologically unpleasant smell into my nostrils. I find myself taking shallower breaths.

'If the two of us could only swap noses,' I begin, and then notice the censor inside me stirring from its lengthy slumber. It seems to be warning me: *You shouldn't make references to other people's body odour, even as a joke.* I reply mentally to this attempt to silence me: *But this American might actually know of some way we can swap our noses or sense of smell. If Max and I could do that, and he could experience the world as it smells to a Japanese woman, it might give him a better shot at building a healthy long-term relationship with one of them in the future, thereby contributing to his happiness.*

The censor seems to accept this, and so I go on. 'If the

two of us could only swap noses, Max, I feel like all sorts of problems would be solved at once.'

The interview lasts around two hours. Once my guest has left, with the room still suffused with the odour of another human, I carry out my pre-work routine, the one that starts with Pilates and ends with my mantra. I steady my breathing and, one by one, replay the questions and answers that were criss-crossing the room just moments before, translating them into Japanese in my head. *I regret ever designing the Dōjō-tō . . . I am weak, and I knew my own weakness, but I failed to control my desires . . . I should never have lent my support to a project that, deep down, I didn't agree with . . . I had no interest in the peace and dignity of all humanity – I just didn't want anyone else to get the job . . . All my mistakes can be traced back to one source: the way I used words to deceive myself . . . In that sense, it's only natural for society to blame me . . . So, yes, I will no longer be taking on any offers of work from the outside world . . . If I ever design another building, it will be a one-hundred-per-cent Sara Machina-funded project, in accordance with the will of Sara Machina alone.*

As I double-check whether my responses survived this change of language with their meaning intact, I also inspect them for evidence of tampering by any will other than my own. If any such interference has taken place, then in accordance with whose will might Sara Machina have said these things, and for what purpose? When my thoughts have gone as far as they can, I start posing my questions to AI-built, responding to each answer with another question. As our words fly back and forth, dusk begins to fall over the city.

In the corner of my eye, the National Stadium and Tōkyō-to Dōjō-tō light up simultaneously. The harmony between the two massive structures is total. I designed the tower this way – it was the idea that won me the competition – so it shouldn't surprise me, but it's as if the two structures are secretly conversing with one another. As I listen to their quiet whispers, I suddenly find it hard to believe I have really been alive in this world for forty-one years. I can't shake the feeling that ever since I was a fourteen-year-old Maths Girl, the same cycle has simply been repeating itself over and over. As though all I've ever done is exchange question and answer, question and answer, endlessly piling up words as if there was no tomorrow – only for them to be washed away, the moment they leave my mouth, by waves whose timing and size I am unable to control. So what, exactly, is the point of all this? For who, or what, has Sara Machina been taught to use language? Suddenly exhausted, I close my laptop and then turn off the power to my brain. I decide to listen only to what my parched throat and empty stomach are telling me to consume at this point in time.

At the Aoyama curry restaurant about a twenty-minute walk from the hotel, I drink two glasses of craft beer, eat a beef curry and a curry bun, then return the way I came. The rain that has been falling since morning is coming down harder now, and the wind is too strong for my umbrella to be of any use. I am the only person walking through the green space of Meiji Jingū Gaien. I remove my cap and sunglasses. The whole of Tokyo is a dreamlike white blur. All I can make out is the tower carving the leaden sky in two, the only object that still seems to be firmly attached to the earth. Was it always this tall, I wonder, as if the tower had nothing to do with me, and gaze steadily at the structure's perfection. Like some proud conspirator convinced it is too early to reveal his true form to humanity, the tower stubbornly hides its sky-rending pinnacle in a veil of rainclouds. The energy-efficient light coming from the windows spaced evenly all the way up its sides is almost blindingly intense. Its form and texture are, as far as these structures we call 'towers' go, exceedingly close to the solution I've always been looking for. And yet I'm not satisfied. Once I've put that feeling – the vague suspicion that *I am not satisfied* – into words, there's no going back. Yes, the tower is the perfect answer to the question asked by the National Stadium. But I can't shake the feeling that within that answer lurks another question. Even if nobody has managed to imagine it yet, there is another building that needs to be built in this city. What sort of building? What will be its shape, its structure? With what thoughts will it be filled? What will they name it? If the tower I'm gazing at is really a question, then it's one that only I am capable of answering.

I let my feet wander wherever they desire and find myself standing in front of the Sympathy Gate. But the rusty iron fence that used to surround the Gyoen gardens has been replaced with a concrete barrier through which even insects would struggle to squeeze, and sneaking in appears basically impossible. In any case, the gate is surrounded by dozens of raincoat-clad policemen and security guards, each staring out with a severe glint in their eyes. Maybe there was some sort of disturbance in the tower today, or yet another bomb threat, or maybe this is how tight the security always is these days. If I were to ring Takt, he might come out with his staff ID and escort me into the tower. With this optimistic thought in mind, I get out my phone and call him.

'Takt?'

'Machina-san?'

'Yeah, it's me. I had my interview with Max Klein earlier. In that hotel by the Gyoen gardens.'

'Ah. I'd forgotten that was today.'

Here we are, thirty years into the twenty-first century, with the majority of jobs replaced by AI, and yet a human voice channelled through an electronic device still sounds exactly like you'd expect that to make it sound: completely devoid of warmth. Instead of focusing on technology that made AI talk like a human, shouldn't we have been trying to work out how to recreate real human voices remotely, right down to the slightest breath? As I listen to the voice coming from my phone, I find myself roughly calculating the economic benefits of this technological brainwave.

'Are you staying there at the moment, then? The place with the restaurant on the ground floor? With the waiter who's the spitting image of your dead cousin . . .'

'That's right. Though he doesn't seem to work there any more.' As I speak I lift my face to the distant sky and focus my gaze on a single point in the thick cloud where the tower's pinnacle presumably lurks. 'Actually, right now, I'm standing in front of the building you call home. I don't even have an umbrella. The wind's so strong it feels like it might knock me over. Poor me, right? But the gate's surrounded by security, and I can't sneak in.'

'Of course you can't. It's not like the old days.' The phone does a decent job of picking up the sound of Takt laughing. Unlike me, he seems to be standing in a very quiet room.

'Are there always this many of them? It looks like there are police here, too.'

'Police?'

'Yeah. There must be at least thirty of them here at the Sympathy Gate alone.'

'Seriously? That does sound unusual. Maybe something's happened. I was off duty today so I'm a little out of the loop.'

'You sure it's not another bomb threat? What do you do when there's one of those – evacuate everyone from the tower?'

'Yeah, that's what the guidelines say. Once we've confirmed that it's not a prank.'

'And if it's not?'

'We move everyone to the National Stadium temporarily. We've done drills.'

'Right. Well, that's a relief.' I pause. 'What were you doing when I rang?'

'I was writing a biography. The biography of an architect.'

'A biography? So . . . you were serious about that?'

'Yeah. But it's tough. I've never written anything this long before. I can't seem to get anywhere – all I do is waffle on about myself instead.'

'Why don't you just type out a few stories from your time with this architect and tell AI-built to rewrite them in the style of a biography?'

'Sure, I've tried that. A few times. The thing is, unless I

describe her exactly the way *I* saw her, it doesn't feel real. I can't quite explain it, but it's like my body won't accept the results. The censor in my head tells me it isn't a biography, just a load of words. No form, no texture, nothing but *fucking text*.' Takt uses English for this last part.

'*Fucking text?* The Takt I used to know never used that sort of language.'

'I picked it up from Max. His mannerisms are super infectious. The guy's basically a walking pathogen.'

'Well, you always were sensitive when it comes to personal hygiene,' I reply, remembering the immaculate soapy fragrance that always emanated from Takt's body. 'Listen, can't you come out here and join me for a moment? I want you to read me some of your words. No *fucking text*. Words that belong to Takt Tōjō and no one else.'

'Sorry. I'd love to, but I'm about to start night duty. Got my rounds to make. How about breakfast at your hotel tomorrow morning? I'll come over to the lobby at seven, and we can eat at that restaurant on the ground floor.'

'I'll still be asleep at seven. Half past?'

'Half past is good.'

'By the way, how's your mother these days?'

'I wouldn't know. But my guess is she's fast asleep somewhere in the tower right now.'

'That's good to hear. Well, see you tomorrow.'

'Yeah, tomorrow. Half past seven.'

Even after hanging up, I feel compelled to stay here, gazing up at the tower while the rain soaks my face. Inside my increasingly waterlogged head I am remembering the plans

I once drew up and imagining that beautifully formed man walking up and down the curved hallways that line the tower's interior. The image of him brings me immense pleasure – so much that I have to close my eyes. I am no longer outside, or inside, anything at all. I, myself, am the structure responsible for those distinctions, and all sorts of individuals with their own lives and emotions are walking in and out of me.

But even as I abandon my body to this endless swelling of pleasure, I can feel something else coming. A vision of the tower's future. I see it now, in all its boundlessness – and yet really it's the most ordinary future imaginable. You wouldn't need to be an architect or a designer of enormous buildings to predict it. It is a future in which Tōkyō-to Dōjō-tō has crumbled to the ground. It might take mere minutes or a hundred years, but the tower will fall. Sooner or later, all buildings do. It is a precondition of their creation, just as death is a precondition of our birth. The tower could meet its end any number of ways. A shift in the earth's tectonic plates might topple it from below. A flying object might hurtle into its side, causing destruction to spread from the middle. A bomb might rip through the structure from above. Or a hand might reach down from the heavens and, with one swing . . .

As I picture the tower's inevitable demise, it strikes me that I too am standing here, my feet planted on the ground, my body rising vertically towards the sky. I begin wondering what would happen if I were to close my eyes and simply remain in this position. How might my body fall? The raging wind might blow me to the ground. The endless rain might soak me into the ground. The midsummer Tokyo sun, emerging from the clouds, might burn me to the ground. Someone who wants to get past might punch me to the ground. A man might force himself on me and push me to the ground. Or maybe I'll collapse from sheer physical exhaustion. I decide that I really will keep my eyes closed, so that I can find out which it's to be. I want to see how the visions in my head measure up to the reality outside it.

But then, in the darkness of my eyelids, I glimpse another future. An entirely new one.

I will not collapse. I will remain upright.

I will stay here with my eyes closed until a certain man passes by. The man will look at me and think, *I must keep this woman standing for all time.* Why he might arrive at this arguably bizarre conclusion, I don't know. Maybe he hates Sara Machina and by keeping her here hopes to make an example of her to the people of Tokyo. Maybe he is just a man with the strange desire to make a woman stand forever in one place. But in a city of fourteen million inhabitants, it doesn't seem unreasonable that one person might arrive at an idea so lacking in logic. After all, the Pyramids of Giza and the Parthenon were not built for reasons that would make sense to everyone. There must have been those who doubted the wisdom of spending such vast amounts of time and resources in the service of gods whose existence was uncertain. Seen through the lens of the distant future, all construction is a form of absurd destruction. In that light, even the National Stadium and Tōkyō-to Dōjō-tō could be viewed as entirely irrational projects that ought to have remained in the realm of the Unbuilt. Just as there's no need to invent some plausible-sounding reason for our birth, the act of construction should not, properly speaking, require the assistance of our hastily cobbled-together words.

The man who wants to keep me here will settle on the idea of building a cast around me and pouring wet concrete into it from above. That way, my very being will be frozen to the ground. I will remain erect, my feet attached to a foundation untroubled by even the fiercest rain and wind. It isn't entirely impossible that this will come to pass. The mere fact that I've expressed it in words suggests its latent possibility. After all, we're talking about something that will happen in the vocabulary of an as-yet unseen future. Maybe the man possesses not only a knowledge of architecture, but also a talent for sculpture, and before I've completely solidified he will begin to shape the concrete around me into something approximating my actual form, creating a statue of Sara Machina. Still, a woman with her eyes closed would hardly represent Sara Machina's true spirit, not to mention running counter to the man's conception of beauty, and so he will also take care to include my eyeballs, carefully moulding them until they resemble their beautiful real-life counterparts. My two eyes will gaze up at the tower, never again to look down. Then, as often happens with people of historical importance, with those great and worthy individuals whose figures are deemed worthy of preservation for future generations, a plaque will be installed at my feet: STATUE OF SARA MACHINA, GAZING UP AT TŌKYŌ-TO DŌJŌ-TŌ.

It doesn't sound like a bad way to be built. In fact, I wouldn't mind standing here like that forever.

Eventually, the people who have gathered around me will begin to spout phrases in my direction, each trying to describe me as they see fit. Of course, what they are saying will be lost on me. All I will know is that the fingers they point at me are all identical, and all convey the same words.

Ecce homo. Behold the woman.

But what if I get the urge to say something back, to answer their monologues with words of my own? If I decide I'd rather walk around this city? If I'm inspired to build something new, something that demands to be built? What then?

The questions are flooding into me now, filling me up from inside, drenching the columns and crossbeams that hold me together, which means I must find the answers. I must go on thinking. For how long? Until this body of mine can remain upright no longer. Until this head of mine, laden with all the words in the world, is dashed against the ground, and I can only watch as heaven becomes earth, and earth becomes heaven.